COWGIRL
Fairytales

Veronica
MACDONALD
AUTHOR

This book is a work of fiction.

COWGIRL FAIRYTALES

Veronica MacDonald

Cover Design and Book Layout
Chuck E Johnson

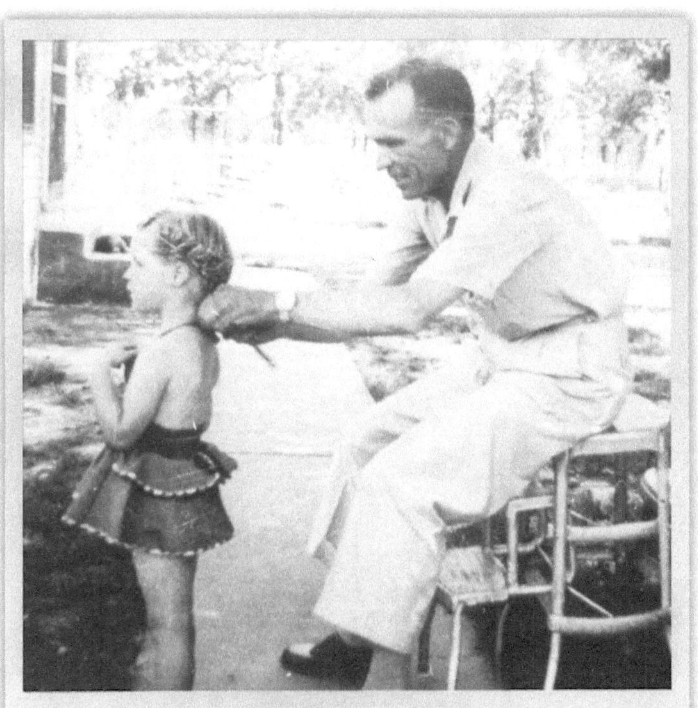

for my sister, Cathy

*And he never had the sense of home so much
as when he felt that he was going there. It was only
when he got there that his homelessness began."*

-Thomas Wolfe
YOU CAN'T GO HOME AGAIN

CHAPTER One

If ever there is a moment to fly in the face of fashion, her job interview at 9:30 on the ninth floor of a glass-walled high-rise building off Fourteenth Street in downtown Atlanta presents just that moment. Determined to buck any conservative trend and to willingly tempt fate in the process, Allie pins a big white fake magnolia on the right shoulder of her Bebe sweater. Might as well be upfront from the word go.

The exit for Fourteenth Street, easier to maneuver since completion of construction, is not the headache it once was. The most disconcerting concern this morning, however, is the prospective job itself: can anyone promise that it won't end up being another endless day that has her checking her watch by 10:30? And, how would one pose that question anyway? Excuse me, but is this the kind of job where noon looms into the next century and the UPS man is the only one in the office who has anything interesting to say? But, what really bums is that today, the day of the interview, the sun would be shining over blooming azaleas; and, there is not a drop of rain falling (as they predicted) in Piedmont Park.

The day she made the interview, weather had been cloudy and work boring. Today, however, she could be walking in Piedmont Park if she only had a dog to walk. She might have said to the administrative assistant in the office, "Can we make the interview for around 4:30 so I can walk my dog?"

Often, during jogs in Piedmont Park, she observes different versions of dog-walking going on: a middle-aged woman with bed-head who wears black slacks and blue t-shirts, walks two small dogs and one Great Dane. The dogs walk as if trained in the art of avoiding leash entanglement; a fit male wearing tight black bike pants runs with his dog running alongside him; a tall, well-coifed blonde woman walks in black pantsuit with a long blue floral scarf around her neck. Her long blonde hair falls straight across the black shoulders of her jacket and she looks at her cell phone the entire time she walks. She twirls when the dog twirls, a vision out of a dog and owner breeding contest. However, most of the dog walkers are random and numerous, which brings to mind precisely the conundrum: who are all those people walking their dogs in the park on days like today anyway? Don't they work? Do they starve for a living? Do they work at night? Are they real people; or are they just extras on a movie set?

After all, it is common knowledge that there are lots of movies being made in Atlanta these days. Rent is cheap (compared to Hollywood); weather is good except that it rains a whole lot more in Atlanta than it does in Hollywood. (Actually, everyone knows it never really rains in Hollywood unless the set designer wants it to.) So, in actuality, there is no practical way to compare Atlanta to Hollywood, nor is there a way to explain away the abundance of idle people walking dogs in Piedmont Park on days like this. No, those people out in the park must have figured out another way to pay the bills. It's plain and simple. She will have to flag one of them down one day and ask them what's what.

Aside from Piedmont Park jogs, Allie often runs some early mornings in upscale neighborhoods of million-dollar homes, their lawns meticulously manicured, little dogs running to the edge of the street barking. Given to avoidant imaginings designed to stave off boredom, Allie thinks that these neighborhoods might be built upon old Confederate soldier battlegrounds. In fact, so adept at fake invention is she that on some mornings when September winds blow just right, she swears she can hear the ghosts of Confederate soldiers moaning.

When in these neighborhoods, she runs in a make-shift fear, clutching closer her powder blue, hooded jacket, its tie strings trailing behind in the tail wind. She is small and trim and having once been a dancer, she is also fleet of foot. Most of the time her hair is flying free, trailing down her back, long and reddish, backlit when the sun shines on it. Her feet hit the pavement in measured steps where sometimes, she slows to a walk, but when she meets a fellow jogger, she begins again to run.

False fantasy aside, maybe these neighborhoods are not built upon ancient battlefields; maybe this sense of foreboding is just a sign of the economic times – a time in history when the need for fairytales becomes more pressing than ever. With the Afghan War fighting for American Idol air time, economic change has happened so fast that people cannot believe it; they keep swimming in the bathtub, thrashing their arms and legs, unable to swim, unable to drown; refusing to believe the water has trickled out. Very gradually during this time, all events have faded to mute, have gotten put on hold; some people have completely shut down. A few people survived the times and other people like Allie just live in a dream world, pretending stupid stuff like, for example, that the plastic picnic table on the deck is really a 1920s wrought iron antique overlooking the French Riviera instead of an Atlanta condo parking lot.

CHAPTER

Two

A severely dressed woman with shoulder-length hair steps around the corner and calls her name, "Allison Gunner," she says with a smile on her face.

"Please, call me Allie." She stands and the flower flops a bit against her sweater. She pats it as if to say, 'Please behave - just for me - just for a few minutes.'

The woman extends her hand and says, "I am Betsy. I am Mr. Booth's assistant. I'm glad you could make the interview at the last minute. How are you this morning?"

"I'm fine," says Allie, "and you?"

"Fine, as well." The woman sighs, "It is difficult to stay inside on such a beautiful day as today."

"Tell me about it," says Allie.

"We'll walk back here," the woman forges ahead with measured, deliberate movement that suggests she is very accustomed to being here in this office and has no real intention of wanting to be outside. She would probably never walk a dog in the park if her life depended on it. Given the chance, she would more likely stay home, take a bubble bath, read a magazine, then go out with friends and have a pomegranate martini.

"Did you have any trouble finding us?" The woman turns slightly around as she poses the question to Allie.

"Nope," says Allie, "Great directions. But then, I'm fairly familiar with Atlanta; been here 15 years." She reflects briefly on how difficult Atlanta had been to maneuver when she first moved from Oklahoma. Nothing ran north or south; sometimes the streets changed names mid-street, and there were about a billion streets named Peachtree Street.

The first time she had gotten lost, and after stopping at a place of business to ask directions from a man sitting behind the desk, she had become confused when he had pointed to the Marriott Hotel and said, "See that old red barn? Turn left there."

Allie had looked out the window and said, "I don't see an old red barn. I see a Marriott Hotel," she had said.

"That's it!" the man had said.

"The red barn? Or, the Marriott Hotel?" Allie had been dumfounded.

Well," he had said, "It's where the barn used to be before the tornado came through." Oh, that explains it perfectly. The man had pushed back in his chair and yelled something into the back room, "Bob, 'member that old saw mill? What's the name of that highway where it used to be?"

A voice had come from the back of the shop, "It's Highway 140 – or it might say Jimmy Carter on the right or Holcomb Bridge on the left."

Yes, Allie had learned early on to resist demanding: "Well, which is it! Is it Highway 140? Or, is it Jimmy Carter? Or, is it Holcomb Bridge?" There was never a definite answer to where something actually was in Atlanta, so she had learned to invest in a map. It was later that she learned how cows had staked out the paths in Atlanta which ultimately became paved highways, and, lord, everyone knows cows walk where they want to, interested more in good grazing than in east versus west. Honestly, a good residential planner would have driven a cow nuts.

Allie follows the woman down the hall toward a back office very much the same way she follows a nurse in the doctor's office, and the nurse, folder under arm, says, 'Follow me; take a seat in here; the doctor will be right with you.' The feeling of doom was very much the same as being in the doctor's office, soon to be the recipient of a flu shot.

Betsy, Mr. Booth's assistant, gestures toward a door to the right and says, "We'll go in here." She peeks inside to be sure no one else is occupying the room and reaffirms, "Yes, in here will be fine. Take a seat."

A conference room is a conference room. Basically, Allie dreads conference rooms. Having been adrift most of her life in the 'corporate world,' she has cut her teeth on conference rooms, wondering the whole time how this came to be. She, the dreamer who could lose herself beneath a tree in the pasture with a book or a poem, had somehow ended up in the restricted world of conference rooms.

Once seated, Betsy opens a folder that holds a resume and other papers. "Allison," she begins, "Let me just ask you a few questions."

Allie straightens in the chair and crosses her legs. She looks at her shoe, black with a gold star stud pattern on the toe of the shoe. The point of the toe makes her leg look long and slim. She is basically slim all over; small and thin; on the short side.

"So," begins Betsy, "how long has it been since your last position with," - she studies the resume; turns it over, shifts through some other papers in the folder she holds on her lap.

"Well," interrupts Allie, "I am actually still employed there."

Betsy lowers her head a bit and peers intently at Allie over the top of her glasses. In truth, she is probably younger than she had appeared when first she rounded the corner in her stiff suit. Caught off guard this way she almost looks vulnerable as she listens carefully and proceeds to form in her mind the next question in the interview. She opens her mouth, but closes it and rubs her lips together, evenly distributing her lip gloss before she proceeds with a question that now seems to be more clearly formulated. "I assume,--" she looks down again at the resume, "I'm assuming your company knows you are looking for employment elsewhere?"

Okay, here it goes. What would be the correct answer; the final answer? Should the answer be: they don't pay me enough! - Or, yes, they know I'm here and are saying good riddance! - Or, no, they have no idea where I am today - Or, no, but I think the company might be secretly going out of business - Or, no, they don't know I'm not at work today because half the time they never know I'm there anyway - Or, no, they don't know I am out looking because they don't realize how much I hate working there instead of spending days in the park.

How far out of line would it be, Allie wonders, to simply say: here's the deal - I was bored the day I made the interview; thought I needed a job change when what I really needed to do was just to face up to something.

"Let's just say," begins Allie, "that it is time for a change for me. I believe I have grown in my skills and knowledge, and am ready for progress, and can better use my skills working in an upgraded organization such as your own."

Betsy smiles, blinks her eyes and nods as if to say that she understands perfectly. Looking down inside the folder, she prepares herself for the next question.

"Should you be offered the position, how soon can you report for work?" She asks the question very innocently as though nothing offensive had been said.

"Well, I was thinking... "Allie stops to formulate her thoughts. She had expected fifty million questions to be asked before this one, but now it is time to face reality or cut bait. "I'm thinking that"..Think fast Allie; this woman means business; she doesn't have much time; things are cut and dried here - as cut and dried as they are everywhere these days. People don't have time, you know. Real people don't, anyway. There are letters to open, e-mails to send. There are courier packages to be prepared and received. UPS is on a deadline. So is FedEx. What do you think this is, anyway? A walk in the park? A walk in Piedmont Park? With a dog?

"I'm thinking," continues Allie. Be honest with that poor woman who is just doing her job. Tell her that all you really want to do is shop and party and go to lunch with friends. Tell her you don't need another job and you wish you had never set up this inane interview. "I'm thinking that I need to go home and think about this before I can give you a definitive answer."

"Oh, Really?" Betsy seems surprised. She says 'oh, really' as if to say…Oh, my gosh, look at that clown on that unicycle.

"Well, it's just that I kind of forgot to walk my dog this morning, and I am a little concerned that it might wet the new rugs in the apartment." Allie looks down again at her shoe and her crossed leg, which she has begun to swing unmercifully.

"But, - " at a loss for words, Betsy glances briefly aside and then down at the carpet underfoot - very expensive looking commercial grade carpeting of swirling patterns in earth tone colors. She briefly lays aside the folder containing the resume and the other employment papers on the large mahogany conference table.

"Could I maybe," Allie continues, "just go home, think about it and call you?"

"You want to call me; to call us back?" Betsy struggles to hide her irritation. "How serious are you about this position? You come to us highly qualified, but there are lots of highly qualified applicants. I mean, you know how bleak the job market is just now. In this instance, however, we are looking for someone more mature than most of our applicants, and Mr. Booth felt you might be the right fit."

Did he now? And why is that? Suddenly, like a brisk wind out of the west, Allie seems to have the upper hand in this interview, even though it does feel like a shallow victory.

Maybe she should go home and formulate some questions of her own: how many sunny days may I contract to remain out of the office? What's to be done about the times I cannot bear the traffic to the 14th Street exit? Who goes out and gets lunch, and when; how long is the lunch hour, for that matter?

But the time for honesty has passed and Allie continues the subterfuge that her boredom has instigated: "Yes, I am serious. I need a change and I would be very interested if I was offered the position. I would just like to think about the time frame. That's all."

Betsy stands as if to signal that this interview is over. It is obvious that there are a million questions running through her mind, but it is also obvious that she would rather die a painfully slow death than dare ask any one of them.

Allie takes the elevator down to the main level of the high-rise building and steps outside where she immediately hears the grinding noise of GA 400, which she pretends is simply the roar of the ocean. Curiously, traffic noise and ocean noises sound virtually the same, and pretending may be the only way country girl hearts can survive the big city.

CHAPTER
Three

The phone rings at 9:00 p.m., and that can only be one person: the friend who sleeps until 2:00 in the afternoon and who doesn't get her day officially started until around 3:00 p.m.: Elyquia. Beautiful as an Egyptian princess, Allie's friend Elyquia was not always known by the name 'Elyquia.' Her name at birth was Wanda, but after she left home and married, she changed her name to something that she felt suited her better. The marriage went by the wayside, but the name remained.

"How did the interview go?" asks Elyquia.

Elyquia and Allie, who met at work, once in a far distant past, had become instant friends and remained thus ever since. Allie, white, and Elyquia, half white, half black; they are soul sisters nonetheless. In many ways, the same woman: both mature, ageless, beautiful, still children of mind. Both are hopeful; both have left men who loved them and men who didn't. Both attract men somewhat younger, and, consequently, both are reluctant to discuss age. Both women have one son - beautiful men in their own right - who are married and share, regarding their mothers, a juxtaposition of adoration and horror.

"I went on that stupid job interview today, but I am not taking the job. I have decided to stay put," says Allie.

This does not surprise Elyquia. She understands how certain

creatures can forever be left in the dust, and how the limo bound for success will sometimes make an incidental stop in the desert; then it may take off again before the star of the show can get back on board. Believing in reincarnation as she does, Elyquia admits that it may take another lifetime before another limousine passes by to pick up the star; therefore, the star must remain patient.

"That is probably smart," says Elyquia.

"I am just bored with where I find myself these days," says Allie. "Restless, you know."

"I know the feeling," says Elyquia. "You know I do."

"Well, girl," Allie surveys her chipped fingernail polish, "I need to find a better way to distract myself rather than take up some poor woman's time interviewing people; a woman who is merely doing her job, for heaven's sake."

"You know what," Elyquia giggles when she says this, "We just need to hurry up and get our little business up and running. I know we can make a go of it."

"You really think so?" The thought of marketing a new business gives Allie heartburn; to think that some students actually major in marketing at college presents a frightful thought indeed.

"Yes, I do," says Elyquia. "But that is not really why I called. We can talk about our business later."

Ah, later, a wonderful timeframe, later. Later turns into four years, then five; then, next thing you know you are thirty-five, forty. Allie marvels at people whom she has seen sitting on the front porch watching the world go by, waiting for later, waiting for the preverbal Godot. Sometimes, she drives by them in her car on the way home from work. Sometimes, she sees them while on vacation when she decides to pull off and check out a garage sale in a strange town. These people who sit on the porch watching her, watching the world; they must know something she doesn't.

Elyquia continues, giggling as she speaks, "I called because I have met this guy at a seminar - he is from Arizona and he wants to take me to dinner."

"Hey, that sounds pretty cool!" says Allie.

"Yeah," continues Elyquia, "he seems like a great guy - good looking and all."

"And, so," says Allie, "Go on…"

Elyquia continues, "Here is the thing: I want you to come and check him out for me. See what you think."

"Sounds good, and how am I doing this?" asks Allie. "Do you have a date for me too? Are we double-dating?"

"No," Elyquia laughs. She laughs in spurts; laughs in phrases. Sometimes she laughs as if the punch line were in the middle of the joke. She is such a child even though not of a child's age. Some people have theories about people and their spiritual age, which goes like this: some people seem to have been born old while others seem to have never matured. Elyquia is still a child with a child's wonder and faith.

"I just want you to clandestinely check him out. We are meeting at Chowie's Club, and I thought maybe you could sit at the bar a few stools down, and just observe the two of us," more laughter follows.

"You mean, act like I don't know you," says Allie.

"Exactly," says Elyquia.

"But, the whole time, I am just observing how he reacts to you," Allie clarifies.

"You got it," says Elyquia.

"Well, you little sneak," says Allie. "Actually, that sounds like fun."

Leave it to Elyquia - always figuring out a way to make the shoe fit her foot. Allie looks down at her frayed sweater, and vows that, very soon, she MUST stop shopping at Goodwill. How has she become such a hound that she has begun to buy her clothes at Goodwill? Maybe it started as a way to buck the mall trend; except now, everyone shops at Goodwill. Their store, packed with millions of garments, color-coded for fast selection for people-on-the-go - blacks together, pinks together - the catch is this: in the store the garment looks awesome; she finds Ralph Lauren; she finds Calvin Klein. However, once home under harsher lights, stains surface and sweaters pill. Cuts, rips, wrinkles, and frays all manage to rear their ugly heads during the drive home from the Goodwill store. The clothes literally seem to have deteriorated in the car.

"Elyquia," says Allie, "I think your idea is sound. It amounts to this, I guess: I don't want to go to a bar and sit on a stool and have to ward off old drunks. Worse even, I don't think I can afford more than two expensive drinks. You know I don't drink anyway."

"So, have a Coke, Allie." This truly seems important to Elyquia - she, a beautiful woman who still believes in fairy tales, too.

"Okay," says Allie, "I suppose I could take Richard with me. He really doesn't look or act gay, do you think?"

"Richard, your decorator?" asks Elyquia.

"Yeah, but he's my friend, too," says Allie. "I don't think he will object, unless he thinks I am trying to ask him on a date so I can 'reform' him."

Elyquia begins to laugh and to fit a few words in between the laugh spurts, as she does: "You….ooo…are…fu..nny, Allie. He.e.e. won't…mind. He will be helping out a friend of…yours…"

"It's really not all that funny," says Allie. "You've never seen him mad; I have!"

"Oh, Allie, no, I think it is a fabulous idea!" says Elyquia. She is happy; she waxes dramatic; she begins to talk about her guy from Arizona. She tells about how they met; how their eyes met 10 states away; the improbability of it all; how fate works; how the universe works; the full moon; the waning moon… on and on.

"Elyquia," says Allie, "Do you think you're going to fall in love again?"

"I am hopeful," says Elyquia. "Always hopeful. I never give up on anything, Allie, until it's over!"

Allie persists, "Looking back, Elyquia, do you think you were ever really in love? Or, merely in infatuation?"

"Of course, I have been in love," says Elyquia.

"Well then, what happens to it?" asks Allie. "When things break up, don't you ever ask yourself if maybe the foundation was faulty? If it might have been built on a false premise? A stupid dream?"

A long pause, not exactly silence, looms like a pre-tornado vortex on the other side of the phone line. Love seems to be a taboo subject for mature women who marry young, stars in their eyes, believing in happily ever after. The children come, the challenges, the bologna sandwiches. Sometimes a few men come and go, who frequently morph into the same man: the man who changed his behavior, the man who became violent, that man who was, in actuality, boring with all his baseball and football nonsense in front of the TV.

"Allie, you're depressed again, aren't you?" asks Elyquia.

"I'm okay," says Allie. "It's just the usual questioning that I do."

"Please, don't become cynical. Just because love changes, doesn't mean it never was. I really don't know what happens to it. I don't have all the answers, but I haven't given up," says the Elyquia-child.

If it were any day other than today, Allie, who has a secret, may have given up on love too. After all, most people do come to their senses eventually. Other people merely adjust to monotony and move to the suburbs. On second consideration, maybe the resolution to mellow malaise is to simply move away from the city. After all, to hear local newscasters tell it, people are asphyxiating in the big city of Atlanta anyway, choking on pine pollen and exhaust fumes. Some mornings the weather girl actually says, "Don't go out of your house today; the air is dangerous." No one, however, has been known to really stay home just because the weather girl said so. People have to go to work and make money so they can go shopping and look like the successful people they think they are. These people die while driving to work in Atlanta traffic, not while breathing the code-orange toxin-tainted air. Silly newscasters!

CHAPTER
four

Richard walks into the bar, fists shoved into his pockets. He is berry brown from working in the yard, and the white polo, contrasted against his skin, makes him look even more deeply tan. He squints in the dark, pulls off his sunglasses and lets them flop onto the white shirt where they dangle from the stringed eyeglass holder, the string's colors matching his madras shorts.

"You're mad, aren't you?" says Allie.

Richard shakes his head and shrugs, right shoulder towards his ear, "No, I'm not mad."

"What's the matter, then?" she asks.

"Well, I mean, how would you feel! People are starting to accuse me of being straight!" says Richard. "My friends think I'm going back into the closet - the other closet, if you get my drift."

"Oh, Richard!" Allie says.

"Well, I'm just saying. How would you like it if people thought you were a lesbian?" He seems genuinely upset.

"Richard, that's just ridiculous!" says Allie.

"Well, it's not only you. I have been hanging out with Margo, helping with her kids' birthday parties, shopping for her husband's clothes. I can't tell you how many of my friends I have run into who actually avert their eyes when they see me lately," says Richard.

"Poor Richard," says Allie. "Has too many people pawing at him."

"It's not really funny," says Richard.

"Okay," says Allie. "Let's just complete this one assignment; I won't ask you to do me any more favors."

"Besides, I have no business in a bar; you know I can't drink with the meds I'm taking," he says, hands still shoved in his pockets.

"So, just have a Coke! I'm probably not going to drink either," she says. "You're making this way too complicated. It's just a fun little evening where we are going to hang out at the bar, check out Elyquia's new date and see what we think."

Slowly, he is making his way towards the bar, looking around, trying to find a menu posted somewhere in the bar.

"Sounds like there's gonna be no red wine for you, then," he says, looking up at the menu that hangs on the wall behind the bar.

"No red wine; probably not; depends how long the night goes," she says.

Richard spots a plate of chicken wings coming out of the kitchen and his mood changes. "I could have a beer and some wings, I guess." His facial tension softens at the sight of the food and the beer, and he walks toward a barstool down at the end of the bar. After looking both ways and over his shoulder, he sits.

"So, you'll have a beer? Yes? A little alcohol after all?" asks Allie.

"Yeah, wings and beer; actually sounds good," says Richard.

"There you go," she swats his shoulder and takes a seat beside him.

Richard squirms on his barstool and looks uncertainly toward the door, "So, again, what exactly are we doing here?"

"We are spying. We have to decide if Elyquia should have a second date with this guy," says Allie.

"Where are they?" Richard turns around on his barstool and looks in the same direction Allie has been looking.

"Obviously," says Allie, "they aren't here yet."

"This is probably a very idiotic question, but why can't she have a date with the guy and decide for herself if he likes her?" Richard asks.

"Well, Richard, it is difficult to explain, but just trust me when I say: it doesn't work that way," says Allie.

"Figures," says Richard.

"I needed you to help me so I don't come in here and get

sidetracked with people thinking I came in here to get picked up," Allie says.

"Oh, you people. Everything is so complicated, when it should be so simple," says Richard.

Allie breathes and focuses on her breath like a yoga stance or like a pre-hypnotic recession. She has no argument; Richard is logically correct; he simply doesn't understand illogical complications.

"Really seems like a lot of trouble to me," he continues. "What makes her so sure he is even going to ask her on a second date?" he says, his linear logic already looking for a way out of the assignment.

"You are angry, Richard," says Allie.

"No, I'm not. I'm just wondering how it is that you and I are qualified to know whom Elyquia should date." He is definitely annoyed.

Allie ponders the validity of his question. "I don't know....... body language maybe," she says.

"When did she meet this guy?" asks Richard.

"I'm not sure. She didn't say; only that she met him at a convention," says Allie.

"Uh-oh... married! That's easy. We just have to look for a wedding ring suntanned onto his left hand. That's all I need to see. Of course, we would literally have to walk over and stare at his hand in the dark," Richard says, his tone becoming more caustic every second.

"Not so fast," says Allie.

"So, body language, huh. And when did you become the body language expert? Been reading up on the subject?" Richard flags the waiter.

"Little stuff… f she messes with her hair, she is flirting… if he…" Allie trails off.

"I thought we were checking him out," Richard fidgets on the barstool and glances nervously behind him as if he is unsure where he should look.

"… if he fiddles with his tie, he is trying to impress her…" she says. Richard looks disgusted as Allie continues: "If his eyes dilate, that is a sign that he really likes her."

"Now, wait a minute," says Richard. "How the hell, may I ask, are we supposed to see in this dark place, sitting half-assed across the room, if this guy's eyes dilate or not!"

"I don't know. Come on, Richard. You know what I mean," says Allie.

"All I can say is get ready! You owe me big time for this."

"That's fine," says Allie.

"No, I'm serious. I'm not whistling Dixie," Says Richard. "Why don't we think about going to your beach house next weekend?"

Allie giggles, "Whistling Dixie?"

"Or something," continues Richard. "Go to Savannah. Go antiquing," he leans back on the barstool.

"Did you really say 'whistling Dixie?" She pokes Richard, but he ignores her.

"Yeah, we could go to the beach," he continues.

"That sounds like fun, actually," says Allie.

"I have to find a piece of furniture for a client, anyway," Richard says, his voice beginning to calm down.

"We can do that; we can go to the beach for the weekend." Allie fumbles her napkin; it falls to the floor; she steps off the barstool to retrieve it.

"I haven't been able to find anything suitable for this client here in Atlanta," he continues, his mind momentarily diverted from bar-spy to interior design.

A good-looking black man enters the bar, looks around; he takes a seat in a corner across the room.

"Richard!" Allie pokes him with her elbow. "Look behind you! That might be him! Keep your eye on him while I visit the ladies' room."

"Humph," says Richard, without turning around.

Allie leaves Richard at the bar and makes her way to the ladies' room which is beautifully renovated with an earth-tone speckled granite countertop and green glass sinks. There are cotton cloths instead of paper towels in the bathroom, and they are rolled and stacked in a wooden wall crate which has been affixed to the wall.

The restroom door opens and Allie sees Elyquia enter the restroom.

"Did you see him, Allie?" Elyquia sounds as if she is dizzy and out of breath.

"Elyquia, you look beautiful!" exclaims Allie.

Elyquia is one who can go overboard on her fashion because she is such a smashing presence that the clothes have unspoken permission to enter the room before she does, as if in preparation for the main event.

"You think?" Elyquia looks down at herself as if her lap would adequately present the entire picture. Her hair, jet black and long, past the shoulders, falls in soft curls. She wears a red, low-cut, somewhat full at the hemline, jersey dress. Her shoes are so high and stacked that Allie thinks she may have to help Elyquia back to the table, thus blowing her spying efforts.

"How do you walk in those?" asks Allie.

Elyquia begins her laughing-in-spurts laugh, "You know what," she laughs, "I don't know. I just bought them."

Allie looks at herself in the mirror. Her hair falls past her shoulders with its permanent side part, courtesy of a cowlick. She is not dressed as one going out, though she will soon be dressing better because she has met a new man, whom neither Richard nor Elyquia knows anything about. Having a secret warms her.

"This is so great of you and Richard to do this for me," says Elyquia.

"Well, he's not too happy about it, but he'll live," says Allie.

"Tell him I appreciate it," says Elyquia.

"I'm going back out," says Allie. "Have no fear. Richard and I are on it." Allie leaves Elyquia still laughing and surveying herself in the mirror, retouching some of the curls that have fallen around her face.

CHAPTER five

It soon becomes evident to Allie that she and Richard have positioned themselves at the bar with their backs turned to Elyquia and her newfound-friend-from-Arizona; that in order to properly spy, they will be required to occasionally turn around, crane their necks, and stare into the back corner more than would be normal for two people at a bar who are supposedly having fun.

"I'm starting to get a crick in my neck," says Richard. "I could probably tell you that he is just away from home playing around. I don't think I need to look at him anymore."

"Not so fast," says Allie. Yet, secretly she believes that this preoccupation with trying to control destiny isn't the entire truth of the matter. Lives are already preplanned aren't they? Pre-positioned in the maze, the true lessons in life happen during the waiting to go through the motions, the bumping into walls, the falling down, the getting up again and gazing occasionally into a distorted mirror until finally gaining the courage to say: This is not really me. This is just a distortion of me; I am somewhere else in this maze and I must be about finding myself. Then comes death. Plain and simple.

Allie looks over at Richard and finds him more engaged than ever with his chicken wings. He eats as if he is about to starve; matter of fact, he is so thin, maybe he really is starving all the time.

"Richard, do you diet?" asks Allie. "Or are you just naturally thin?"

"No," Richard's voice cracks, "I can't keep weight on. Why would I be dieting?"

"It was just a thought; just an observation." Allie remembers the first time Richard told her how he came out to his family. He told her of his childhood; when he knew he was gay - a matter she vowed never to repeat. She had told him things about her dead husband that she could tell no one else. There were even things about the husband that she could never tell anyone, not even Richard.

"Oh, look Richard, he is touching her cheek," Allie sneaks a peek into the back of the room while she glances at Richard washing chicken wings down with beer.

"That's it; I'm telling you, the guy's married." Richard shrugs his shoulders, but does not turn around to look.

"I don't care about that. We are merely supposed to see if we think he likes her," says Allie.

"Allie, don't be naive. All guys like women."

"Except you," says Allie.

"That's not the point really. Is it?" Richard frowns. "What the heck, I mean – what! Does she plan to marry this guy!? What's the big deal! I don't get it. Why can't they just go on a date and be done with it?"

Allie stares at Richard. He really doesn't get it. How could he know anything about this? He couldn't. He just wants to finish his wings in peace, maybe have another beer; then go home and start organizing his closet.

"I think maybe we should move to a table with a better view." Allie looks behind her to see several empty tables that would afford them an arrow-straight view of the situation.

"Now, that is really going to look dumb," says Richard. "I pick up my wings and beer; you, schlepping your wine and maybe this bowl of peanuts, move to a table; then, proceed to stare straight at them. He will probably think we are the detectives hired by his wife to follow him around while he's out of town." Richard waves his beer mug in the air while he talks; then, he takes a swig and sets the mug back down.

"Maybe we could summon the bartender; ask him politely if he would, clandestinely, move this stuff for us while we go to the restroom; then, when we come back, we could sit at the table very nonchalantly, as if we have been there all night. I don't think the guy would notice," says Allie.

"Oh, my lord, what would you do without the restroom!" says Richard.

"Or…..or…..oh, I have a better idea. Why don't we get up and dance? We could dance by the table once in a while. Maybe even catch a little of their conversation," says Allie.

Richard looks directly at Allie for the first time tonight. "Exactly how much did she pay you to perform this assignment?"

"Richard!" says Allie.

"No, I'm serious, Allie; how much?"

This is, indeed, a good question. What is the vested interest in Elyquia's love life? How many times have the girls been down the man road since Elyquia's divorce and Allie's widowhood? Is this what all women do? Or, is this what mature women do? No, no, Allie is convinced there is no difference between the two. Womanhood knows no age when it concerns matters of the heart. There is no dividing line, no stopping point. Mature love is as magical as love at the Senior Prom.

"You know, Richard, everything isn't always merely a matter of dollars and cents."

"Allie," says Richard, "you are making me really nervous. I would rather be stuck with hot needles than get up and dance with you."

"I know, I know. The feeling is mutual, actually." Allie rests her chin on her elbow and stares out the window. Night is making its appearance. A crowd forms at the door, their silhouettes hang as ghosts against street lights behind the glass door. A little noise is happening in the street - not loud noise, just laughter and muted voices, like so much clutter.

"Richard, I have a confession to make to you," Allie says bluntly.

Richard puts his hand to his head and closes his eyes, as if to say he can absolutely take no more of her foolishness. She wonders if the beer has given him a headache, if maybe the alcohol is, indeed, interfering with his medication. He takes a slow, deep breath through his open mouth, as merely inhaling through the nose at this point might give him no oxygen whatsoever.

"Shoot," he says, visibly braced for verbal turbulence. "Go ahead; say it. I'm ready!" His eyes are still closed.

"I think I have met my third husband," she says.

Richard looks stunned. He puts down his chicken wing, wipes his fingers on his napkin, and turns to face Allie. He closes his eyes then opens them again wider than before and speaks so loudly that the bartender looks up. "What!"

Even the handsome guy sitting with Elyquia in the darkened, back corner of the bar, looks toward them.

"Yeah, I keep running into this guy...." she continues.

Richard glances out the bar door as if to plan a rapid escape. "Allie, I just never know what is going to come out of your mouth," he says.

The two sit in silence with only white background noise between them. She twirls her wine glass, watching the purple liquid swish around in its stem-topped bowl.

Richard recovers and after a long moment, he speaks. "So you keep running into him. So, what else? Tell me more." He looks at the ceiling as he waits for the answer.

"Oh," says Allie, "it is too soon to be any more specific. Just that we keep bumping into one another and it feels like it is meant to happen."

Richard, having lapsed into his pragmatic stance, looks at the ceiling as he poses his next question, "So, he has asked you out and everything?"

"No," says Allie.

Richard continues to look at the ceiling. "I'm not going to make a big deal of this."

"A big deal of what?" asks Allie.

"Of how idiotic it sounds that you are getting ready to marry a man who hasn't even asked you out." Richard pushes away his dish of stripped chicken bones; he deposits another empty chicken wing bone onto his dish; lifts his beer mug and drinks. "I think you should just take a valium and go to bed," he says. "This will probably pass."

"That is just the point, Richard, I don't really want it to pass," says Allie. "I kind of like this guy."

A crash sounds back in the kitchen. The bartender looks over his shoulder before he disappears into the back. But nothing comes of it. No more noises follow. Even the few customers in the bar seem not to notice. Soon the bartender reappears, shop rag thrown over his shoulder, and resumes dunking glasses into soapy water then into bleach water.

"I know," says Richard, "but liking this guy and finding your third husband are miles apart. That's all I'm saying."

Snow is falling in Allie's heart. She can hear it, actually. She can hear snow falling above the noise of the bar and above the noise of the crowd at the door as they swing wide the door, walk into the bar, and occupy three of the empty tables. She can even hear it above the music that has now been cranked up louder than before - 'all I wanna do is have some fun - I gotta feelin' I'm not the only one - all I wanna do is have some fun before the sun comes up over Santa Monica Boulevard.'

CHAPTER
Six

Richard and Allie drive to the beach early the next morning, and when they arrive, they find that a party invitation has been taped to the back door of Allie's beach house.

> COME TO A 4TH OF JULY PARTY
> AT 1274 BAY STREET
> 7:00 P.M. SHARP
> BOOZE PROVIDED

"Hey, Richard, here's a party we can go to!" Allie says.

"When is it?" He is standing on the back step behind her.

Allie hands the invitation to Richard and digs in her purse searching for house keys. "July 4th," she says.

"That's in two days. Who is this? Anyone you know?" Richard asks.

"Not directly. I think she is a friend of my neighbor," Allie points across the street. "Jean; moved here from St. Simon. She got a divorce; got a younger boyfriend. She knows lots of people here already."

Richard unloads things from the van while Allie unlocks the back door of the house. Richard walks through the open door and heads toward the guest bedroom as comfortably as if he lives here himself. He has visited many times since the death of Bob, Allie's second husband. It is necessary to get away from Atlanta often - the non-stop traffic, the brown scorched grass, the unrepentant jackhammer.

"Allie, the house smells musty. You should really leave the AC on all the time, or at least the ceiling fans." Richard looks around the room as he talks.

The house feels like an ancient soul. There hangs the silk screen carp fish painting Allie found in a flea market and Bob convinced her to buy. On the bookshelves either side of the fireplace sit family mementos from her parents' day, including a hot beer set with cherubs on the lid. The set was brought back from Germany by her father after World War II. There are sketches and finger-painted pictures created by Allie's grandchildren, which pictures graduated from the refrigerator into picture frames. A few dead Palmetto Bugs lie, feet up, on the kitchen floor.

"Let's finish unpacking, have lunch, and drive to Savannah," says Richard. "I want to visit Mark; but I'll call first. Make sure he doesn't have plans."

He pulls his cell phone from the pocket of his shorts, hits a few buttons and after a bit, begins to speak. "Mark," a pause; then, "it's Richard. We're here, Allie and I, at the beach house. We're talking about driving over. Will that work for you?" He listens, "Yeah, right now. That okay?" Then he says, "Perfect. Bye." He taps his cell phone and returns it to his pocket.

After finishing unloading the van, Allie checks the front porch to be sure the furniture is still intact. It is, but the front porch is very dusty from cars going by; she will have to clean up the porch first thing in the morning before they can sit out there. They walk through the house once and then the two of them, departing through the back door, lock it up again.

Inside the van, they make the 30-minute drive to Mark's house in Savannah.

Mark's house is sparingly, yet tastefully furnished. Three low dark wooden tables with steel legs sit side-by-side in front of a sprawling brown sectional. Mark has been watching television, but stands and begins to return pillows to their proper places while Richard and Allie make their way into the room.

"Allie, look," Richard points to the wall behind the sectional, "That is Ralph Lauren Cowgirl Blue paint that I want you to use in your bedroom."

Allie looks at the wall, but it isn't the paint color that catches her eye. She is fascinated by a large abstract painting of black, brown and orange splotches. It is centered squarely over the living room sectional, and is stunning, displayed as such, against the soft blue wall.

"You remember, don't you, the Cowgirl Blue paint?" Richard persists.

"Oh, yeah; I like it; I do. It looks good in here, that's for sure," says Allie.

"Thanks," says Mark. He picks up the remote; flips off the big screen television that hangs on the wall opposite the sectional; extends an outstretched arm, and invites Richard to come closer.

While they hug, Allie turns away, giving the two their privacy. She walks to the French doors and looks out onto the deck that leads down to the Koi pond. She doesn't even want to think about the Koi pond. It hurts her heart to watch the fish jump out of the water with their big round hungry mouths wide open, begging for food. There are too many fish in the pond and she is convinced they are starving. When they hear footsteps on the deck, they all swim toward the deck and practically jump out of the water. There seems to be more and more fish each time she comes; they keep multiplying; keep growing larger; keep begging for food. Someplace, she doesn't remember where, she heard that if Koi get too hungry, they just eat each other. That doesn't sound too comforting, either.

Mark goes into the kitchen, pours Coke Zero over ice into three highball glasses; gives one to Richard, and taps Allie on the shoulder, prompting her to turn around.

"Here," he offers. "Oh, thanks," she takes the glass.

Mark raises his glass in a salute and they drink almost in unison, "Good to see you; both of you."

"God, is it hot outside!" says Richard.

"So, what chyall up to?" asks Mark. "Just bumming or what?"

"I'm collecting on a huge debt," says Richard as he grins for the first time today, "and what better place to do so than at the beach."

"A huge debt, huh?" says Mark, "I can only imagine what you two have gotten yourselves into this time, but I'll be damned if I'm gonna ask."

"Don't," says Richard, "you'd never even believe it!"

Mark takes another long sip of the cool liquid and stares down the side of the glass at the two of them, "Well, sit down anyway."

"So," Richard addresses Mark as he sets his drink on a coaster, "what is going on with you?"

"Uh, when have I talked to you last?" Mark frowns as he thinks. "Had I gotten back from Italy yet?"

"I think so," says Richard. "You were thinking about buying that foreclosed house down the street."

"Oh, yes, that," Mark plumps the pillow behind him, "I decided against that, after all."

"Did you!" exclaims Richard.

"Uh-huh, I did; way too much money going out. I'm tired right now, anyway," says Mark.

"I know what you mean. I'm not working much these days. I have a few clients, but most everyone is pulling back; tightening their belts," says Richard.

"Things are so weird," says Mark. "Business is way down; people are moving; I see nothing but old people out walking. They got their hats on; they got their shorts on - their legs as pale as that curtain," he points across the room to a pair of blonde linen curtains that frame a large floor-to-ceiling window.

"Good. Maybe they'll get their fat asses back in shape," says Richard.

"I think that's the idea," says Mark. "Allie what's up with you; still at the same job?"

Before Allie can formulate her thoughts, Richard interjects, "Allie is getting married."

"Yeah?" Mark straightens himself and scoots forward on the sectional, signaling sudden, rapt attention, "Anyone we know?"

Allie turns her head and stares straight out the window to the right. She can see a purple Rose of Sharon struggling in the sun. It has grown quite tall for a Rose of Sharon and it sways in the breeze as if it is waving to her. Beyond that, sits another house that has been painted an Adobe yellow, such a brilliant color combination to behold on a hot July day: purple and yellow.

Soon, it will be her birthday and she doesn't even know if she wants to celebrate another birthday, ever. She doesn't want to have them, and she certainly doesn't want to celebrate them. She had quit celebrating things after Bob died, because celebrating upon the occasion of death seemed senseless at the time - especially that first Christmas; then, eventually, all the Christmas seasons that followed. One by one, she gave away all her Christmas decorations. She stopped putting up trees; stopped celebrating Christmas altogether. Soon, she ceased to celebrate anything. She learned to endure the candy, the well-meaning, gift-giving friends and neighbors, the cards from relatives and old friends who still lived out west.

"Richard," says Allie, "you're an ass!" But suddenly she laughs. She laughs at the thought of being in love again after 10 years. Yet, this is not something that she cares to discuss right now; or, with these two, at no time, ever, for that matter. She thinks about Elyquia and her new man. She must remember to call her and report the findings, however inconsequential. But what will she say to Elyquia? -No, it didn't look like he was all that interested, but it didn't look like he was disinterested either - Or, Allie could make something up that she knew Elyquia would want to hear such as: He was practically drooling on himself and I predict he will be the one you've been waiting for all your life. Or, she could be perfectly honest and say: Richard and I are so inept at love we wouldn't know it if it walked up and smacked us in the face, so whatever we say, put your money on the opposite.

Allie rises from the chair, "Please excuse me while I visit the powder room." She walks down the hall noting the beautiful silver bird wallpaper on the wall leading to the bathroom. What a decorator Mark is! He had once been the set designer for some traveling theatrical group. Maybe he should still be doing that.

"The powder room," sighs Richard. "That girl has such an affinity for the powder room!"

"Do tell," says Mark.

CHAPTER
Seven

Richard and Allie arrive back at the beach house in time to prepare for the 4th of July party. Fashionably late, they make the party by around 8:30 p.m., and find it in full swing, with people spilling out of the house onto the large front lawn. Painted a pale pink with white wrap-around porches on both the upper and lower levels, the house at 1274 Bay Street is a three-story antebellum home straight out of Gone With The Wind. There are round tables dotting the front lawn, all of which skirt full-length white tablecloths that hang down to lush green lawns below. Lights are strung on poles around a cabana that houses food and alcohol, colas, wine, water and tea. Music comes from inside the house; someone is playing the piano. Music inside the house, music outside the house, all of it, combined with the laughter and conversation on the lawn, reduces everything to a background hum.

Allie wears a strapless white summer dress she had purchased at the Goodwill just because it was too beautiful to leave hanging on the rack for only $5.00. Richard also wears white - a summer suit; he looks very much like Scott Fitzgerald (if anyone really knew what Scott Fitzgerald looked like).

A very beautiful, older woman smiles at them as they climb the steps to enter the house. She is tall, maybe 69 or 70 years of age, with not a wrinkle on her face. She is very pale as though she has never ventured into the sun. Even her hands are unspotted. Making eye contact with the two of them, she smiles widely and says, "Hi-i-i- i-i," stretching out the word until it becomes almost embarrassing. Then she says, "Welcome. Come in and get yourselves a c-o-o-l drink." Allie wonders if she is the owner of the house – the one who is actually hosting the party; but she doesn't ask.

Straight ahead, the house breaks up into four areas. A white baby grand piano sits in the left corner where a man in a black Tux plays, head bent toward the keys, playing without music. A couple of tipsy women and two young couples stare lovingly over the piano at him as if, by osmosis, they might will themselves to become pianists.

In the area in front of the piano, several couples sit eating and drinking using tea tables, coffee tables, and side tables to hold their food and drinks. Oriental rugs beneath are a light cream color with so many other swirls of color that they can blend quite nicely with any food that may be dropped throughout the evening.

Two rooms on the right of the grand hall are also occupied with various groups of people, and in one of the rooms several people are gathered around a game table where a poker game is in full swing. That room is particularly smoky and Allie quickly moves back into the hall away from the smoke. She sees her neighbor Jean, from across the street, the one who had extended the party invitation, and she taps Richard on the arm, "I'll be right back."

Jean is dressed in a black sheath dress which shows off her blonde hair beautifully. She is a bit heavy, maybe 15 pounds heavier than she would like to be, but she looks beautiful in spite of a few pounds. She wears a large white pearl bracelet and big gold hoop earrings. Standing beside her is her young boyfriend, who looks as if he could be her boyfriend, but, actually he looks as if he could also be her son, or at the very least, the houseboy.

The boyfriend glances adoringly down at her cleavage, liking, no doubt, the extra 15 pounds that her husband probably grew to dislike. Allie sees that Jean is talking to those around her; they are enthralled in what she has to say because soon the group breaks out into loud laughter. Maybe she tells a dirty joke. Maybe she talks about her ex-husband's cooking or his golf score. For a brief second, Allie is unsure of herself. Should she walk over to Jean, break into the circle and thank her for the invitation? Maybe she should go somewhere else in the house and join another group. She looks behind her to see that Richard has struck up a conversation with a small circle of good-looking men who are standing with two older, grey-haired ladies.

Someone comes up behind Allie and touches her shoulder, "I think I know you," he says.

She turns quickly, looks into his face and tries to place him. Studying him briefly, she says, "You look familiar to me. I'm sorry; remind me where we've met."

"I'm your neighbor," he says, "Bart - across the street."

"Oh yes, Bart!" She remembers him now. "My neighbor who lives across the street!"

"You're always working in the yard early mornings," he says.

"Yes, doing yard work - when I'm in town. Yep, the yard always seems to need lots of work after it has sat idle for a few weeks," says Allie.

"In fact, you seem to work in the yard non-stop," he laughs.

Bart has a big tattoo on his right arm. She knows this because she saw it the first day he came over to introduce himself. It appeared to be some kind of a military tattoo; it was a big Eagle. Bart could have easily served in Desert Storm. The tattoo is not visible now, though, because he wears a formal coat and pants, no tie.

"So, you are in town for the 4th, I see," he continues.

Although Bart has never mentioned a wife, Allie suspects he is married because she has seen a woman drive a white car into the driveway next door. The day he had walked over into her yard to introduce himself, he had acted like any other overly-friendly man on a mission. They spoke briefly about how he was a contractor, and if ever there was any work she needed done around the house, he would like to be given the opportunity to be her contractor of choice.

"Yes, a friend and I drove down from Atlanta," says Allie.

"Oh?" Bart takes a quick look behind him. Allie is tempted to ask 'Where is your wife?' but that would be mean and she knows it. She looks at his left hand; still, there is no ring. He hadn't worn a ring the day he had first introduced himself, either. That day they had spoken, Elyquia, observing from the front porch of the beach house, had told Allie that his body language revealed he was 'uncomfortable' while they were speaking.

"Yeah, he's my gay friend, Richard. That's him over there,"

Allie nods toward the first room on the left where Richard has now taken a seat and has leaned back quite comfortably onto a camel-backed ball and claw love seat.

"Oh, yes, I think I have seen him before," says Bart. "You have brought him down before. Also, that beautiful black lady; she has come down with you before."

"Yes, Elyquia," says Allie.

"So, how is Atlanta these days?" Bart seems starved somehow for news of big city life. "Is the aquarium as wonderful as they say?"

"It certainly is," says Allie, but this is a lie. She has not gone near the aquarium; yet, she knows it is well-advertised and supposed to be spectacular. It isn't unusual when one lives in towns full of things to do, to do none of the things afforded them.

"I hope to get up there one day to see the aquarium. My daughter wants to go so badly," says Bart.

Alas, he has said it. He admits to some kind of family. Maybe it is his daughter who drives the white car into the driveway; maybe his daughter is ten years old; maybe she is a teenager, even though the woman who drives the white car into Bart's driveway looks much older.

"Say, we should go for a drink sometime," says Bart.

This confirms Allie's gut feelings about Bart. He has been trying to work up to asking her out. But, he clearly has a wife, or maybe she is the housekeeper, or maybe she is a thirty-five, forty-something teenager, which would make Bart at least sixty-something and balding. The fact is: Bart becomes more of an enigma each time they speak. And another, more important fact, is this: it is too late for Bart; Allie has a new man.

"Yeah, just knock on my door someday," Allie says, knowing this will never happen. She smiles and Bart smiles back.

CHAPTER
Eight

Allie hears a tinkling sound and realizes that inside her purse, barely audible above the party noise, her cell phone is ringing.

"Bart," she says, "Could you excuse me for a minute? I think my phone is ringing."

"Oh, sure; good to see you, Allie," he touches her on the shoulder before she walks toward the door, reaching inside her purse for the phone; it will be more quiet outside.

"Hello," she says.

"Allie? This is Elyquia."

"Oh, hi; how are you?" Allie says.

"Did I catch you at a bad time?" asks Elyquia, "I hear commotion in the background."

"Well, I'm at the beach. We're at a 4th of July Party, Richard and I," says Allie.

"Oh, that sounds like such fun," Elyquia holds onto her words as if to taste them, "I wish I could be there."

"Me, too," says Allie, "There are some good-looking guys here." "Well, listen," says Elyquia, "I'll call you back. When are you going to be home?"

"No, no, it's okay," says Allie, "Your call sort of saved me from an awkward situation, as a matter of fact."

"Really," Elyquia says.

"Yeah, Bart, remember him?" says Allie.

"Bart – from across the street?" says Elyquia, "That guy who kept reaching back behind, scratching his neck when you two talked that day in the yard?"

"Yeah, him," says Allie.

"I really think he wanted to ask you out," says Elyquia. "But, something wasn't right."

"It's just me," says Allie, "I'm sort of a misfit. I don't fit in anywhere."

"Yes, you do!" says Elyquia. "You just don't think you do."

"Isn't that the same thing?" asks Allie.

"Oh, my," says Elyquia. "Well, you call me when you get back home to Atlanta."

"No, it's okay," says Allie. "I can talk."

Allie walks out of the house onto the lawn where, off to the side, she finds a table vacant, except for an elderly man and a child. She sits at the table and places her purse in front of her.

"So, how are you and your new man getting along?" asks Allie.

"We're doing g-r-e-a-t," says Elyquia, "I am going to see him again tonight."

"I guess you would like a full report of our findings, Richard and mine," says Allie.

"What did you think?" asks Elyquia, "I didn't get a chance to talk to you. Did you think he was cute?"

"That, he is," says Allie, although she really couldn't remember much about him except that he was tall, and Richard thought he was married.

"What did Richard think?" asks Elyquia.

"Oh, Elyquia, what does Richard know! He wasn't much help; he thought he might be married."

"Why?" asks Elyquia. "Why would he think that?"

"I don't know," says Allie. "I probably should have brought someone with me who would have been a better judge."

"But, I'm more interested in what you think," says Elyquia.

Allie still cannot break it to Elyquia that she and Richard had done a top-notch, super-duper job of failing her in their spying efforts. The two had become too engrossed in the beer, the chicken wings. Also, Allie was more interested in the new man she keeps running into at flea markets. The first time they met, he had asked someone at the counter who she was. Little did he know that the "someone at the counter" promptly told Allie there was a strange man asking about her; who thought she looked sort of like Audrey Hepburn, and asking 'who was she;' and, 'did she come here often;' and, how he thought she was so attractive.

The second and third times they ran into one another accidentally, he had made it a point to speak to her. He had made a casual comment about how they must be 'on the same schedule with their junking,' and, they had both laughed.

The third and fourth times they met, both shopping for that perfect vintage find, he had stopped her, and, looking intently at her while he spoke, had asked how she had been; had she been busy this summer? He had asked other leading questions that might encourage a response beyond common small talk.

The fifth and sixth times they met, Allie had decided these chance meetings must be some kind of destiny.

"Here is what I think," says Allie, "Obviously, he is interested in you because he asked you for a second date. As to whether or not he is married, that is, I suppose, a possibility."

"I have thought about that too," says Elyquia.

"The thing concerning me most is that he is from Arizona. How will you continue much of a relationship when he lives five or six states away?" asks Allie.

"I know," says Elyquia, "He is here in Atlanta on some kind of work assignment for an indefinite period of time, though."

Allie knows Elyquia is trusting and kind, almost naïve. "I just don't want you to get hurt, and, I can see that as a possibility."

Elyquia laughs in spurts between her words, "That's always a possibility, but he is worth the chance, I think."

"Well, those are things only you would know, so I say go for it. Have a great time with him. Who knows where things end up; I certainly don't," says Allie

"Thanks, Allie," says Elyquia.

"Sure," says Allie. "Bye." She puts the phone back in her purse, and rising from the table, she walks over to the cabana to find something to drink, where she sees Jean and boyfriend standing on the lawn in a crowd of people. About the same time Allie sees Jean, Jean sees Allie and advances, with outstretched arms, in her direction.

"A-l-l-i-e," Jean calls as she walks across the yard, "you m-a-d-e it! Come ovah heah! I whant yew to m-e-e-t someone."

Allie walks toward Jean and her boyfriend. The closer she gets, the younger the boyfriend looks. He is tall, tan, has short hair, cute, and the beginning of a beer gut.

Jean reaches out and hugs Allie, "I want yew to m-e-e-t my boyfriend, Carl!"

Allie offers her hand, "Pleased to meet you."

"Likewise," says Carl. He appears shy and somewhat ill at ease.

"I sawh Richard back in th' h-a-o-u-s-e. I'm glahd you browt him. Hope yhall r' havin' f-u-h-n."

"We are; this party is great. I don't really know who is hosting it, but thanks for inviting us," says Allie.

"O-h, it's Evelyn," Jean gestures toward the sky. "She does this every y-e-a-h. Gives her a chance to empty the ole' w-i-h-n cellah," Jean laughs and looks at her boyfriend, "You know Evelyn don't ya' baby? Her 'n 'r sistah own the funeral home downtown."

"Yeah, sure, I know her," says Carl. Jean turns back to Allie, "Have yew f-a-h-u-n-d good thangs ta eat? I'm just c-r-a-v-i-n' oaysteahs; but they're not in s-e-a-s-o-n yet. The s-h-r-i-m-p's guud, though."

"Oh, I'll find something to eat," says Allie.

"Allie, come over heah with me. I want to introduce yew to a deah friend of th' family." Jean takes Allie by the arm and kisses her boyfriend on the cheek, "Be right back, Sugah."

The women walk across the lawn; walk up the steps into the house, and head toward the piano room. The pianist, apparently on a break, has been replaced by a Karaoke Machine. A tall girl in a short skirt stands on a makeshift stage holding the microphone and sings "Jeremiah Was A Bullfrog."

"I hate that song!" says Allie.

"Just ignore her, darlin'," says Jean.

"Oh, there's nothing wrong with her; I just hate that song," says Allie.

"Well, blame it on the piano playuh, for takin' a break." Jean tugs at Allie's arm. They round the corner and Jean reaches her hand out toward an older gentleman with snow white hair and a well-groomed, white mustache. He wears a black tuxedo with black and white shoes, the pairing of which makes him very much resemble a Penguin.

"Dale, come heah," Jean calls to him, "This is my neighbor from across the street; this is Allie."

Dale steps forward rather formally, takes Allie's hand, presses it to his lips and gives her an old-fashioned kiss on the hand.

"My, what a southern gentleman!" says Allie.

"Oh, no, honey. Dale is from New Yoahk. He's an actah from New Yoahk," says Jean.

"Really!" says Allie, "you came all the way from New York to the party?"

"My dear," he begins, and for one split second Allie thinks he is going to say: My deah, I don't give a damn..., but he says, "I live in Atlanta too."

Allie looks at Jean, and Jean says, "He lives in Atlanta now, but he was bawhn in New Yoahk. He's a Y-a-n-k-a-e-e," Jean laughs, "But, I still let him travel in mah circle, don' I sugah?" says Jean.

"Yes," says Dale, "I travel in Jean's circle where I have never been known to miss a good party, have I, Jean?"

"No, darlin'," says Jean. "Dale used to be a cahr salesman in New Yoahk, and now he's an actah in Atlan'a; funny how life wurks aught, isn't it Dale?"

Dale folds his right arm to hold taut his tux as he leans forward to answer Jean's question, "Yes, my dear, life is delightfully hilarious." His smile cannot hide his sophistication.

"A car salesman, huh?" says Allie, "I thought one didn't need a car in New York."

Dale, maintaining his somewhat formal stance, turns only his head as he speaks, "I'm afraid that is a gross misnomer; people drive cars in every town."

Not knowing whether to be offended or entertained, Allie continues her inane conversation, "Can you give me a quick tip on buying a car?"

Not missing a beat, Dale quips, "Never buy a green car; they are the last cars on the lot to sell."

Clearly amused and rushed at the same time, Jean laughs and then turns to Allie, "Now I'm gawhna leave you tue to towk."

Courtesy of Jean's farewell hug, Allie smells perfume that is strong and musty, not light and flowery as one would think a summer evening party perfume might be. It smells more like night and danger; in fact, the more she thinks about it, she remembers the familiar aroma because it is the same perfume Aunt Selda used to wear: Tabu. With the memory of the perfume comes the memory of the advertisement for Tabu. It is of a piano teacher so overcome with emotion for the young lady he is teaching that there on the piano bench, he bends her backward in a passionate kiss.

No sooner has Jean walked away from Allie and Dale than a tall, skimpily-dressed young woman with long shiny auburn hair slinks toward Dale, and puts her arm around his shoulder. She is so much taller than him that she stands almost a head above him. She looks at Allie as she speaks, "Darlin', I wondered where you'd gone off to."

The girl extends her hand toward Allie, "Hi, my name is Tiffany; how are you?"

"Fine. I'm Allie," she says.

So, here we are, thinks Allie; every party has an end and this feels like the end of this party. Dale, who is being gently led away by Tiffany, does a small bow and says, "Very nice to meet you, Allie."

"You as well," says Allie. She smiles and turns around, leaving Tiffany and Dale behind.

CHAPTER

Up 9:30 the next morning, Allie decides to have breakfast on the front porch. While in the process of removing covers from the wicker furniture and sweeping the porch, she sees that a woman is mowing Bart's lawn across the street.

"I knew it, Richard!" She runs to the guest bedroom and knocks loudly on the bedroom door, "Richard, are you awake?"

His voice sounds croaky, "No," he says.

"You have to come outside and look! Bart does have a wife; she is mowing their lawn!"

Allie hears the rustling of bedding beyond the door. "What time is it?" Richard calls.

"It is 9:30, 9:45, almost 10:00," says Allie.

"We were out pretty late, you know." Richard's voice sounds tired.

"Okay, but get up soon; I am making breakfast." She goes into the kitchen and puts on water for coffee. She looks in the freezer – some frozen pizzas, a carton of Cool Whip. She closes the freezer door and opens the refrigerator door; there is bread, butter, individual cans of tomato juice; there is jelly, iced tea in bottles; the pickings are slim.

She toasts two slices of bread, places them on a plate and spoons jelly into a china cup. She cuts a butter stick in half, places it on a plate, and sets both dishes on a big round tray where she adds two coffee cups, a pitcher of milk, two plates, knives and napkins. Carrying the big round tray towards the front porch, she calls over her shoulder, "Breakfast in 10 minutes."

Outside, she sets the food tray on the round glass porch table; then she seeks a peek across the street again at Bart's wife: blue shorts, white sleeveless blouse, shortly cropped brown hair. There are no frills about her; she is just a hardworking woman out mowing her philandering husband's front yard. Granted, Bart did do a great job of remodeling the old house. It has gone from a run-down white bungalow to a pale yellow house with white porch and cedar shingles down the wall of new guest quarters built off the back of the house.

Bart's wife, now with sprinkler in hand, walks behind the house to the backyard. Not only does she mow the lawn, she even waters the lawn. A neighbor joins Bart's wife in the backyard and says something that is muffled and inaudible above cars passing in front of the front porch. Shortly, the neighbor returns from behind the house carrying a couple of plump blue hydrangeas. There you have it: along with everything else she does, Bart's wife has now shared with her neighbor two beautiful flowers raised, watered and cared for by she, caretaker of jerks, doer of spousal deeds.

The screen door to the porch opens, creaking as it goes, and a disheveled Richard steps onto the front porch. By now bird chatter is thoroughly drowned by traffic and lawnmower noise.

Richard takes a seat on the wicker couch, runs his fingers through his hair and grumbles, "Does the entire world mow their lawn on July 5th?"

"Good morning," says Allie. She pours him coffee from the press and hands it to him.

"Thank you; oh, I need cream," he says, handing the cup back to her.

She pours from the little bone china pitcher for a couple of seconds before he says, "That's enough. Thanks."

"Quite welcome," says Allie.

Richard on the sofa, Allie at the table, they sip their coffee in silence. He sets his coffee cup on the table in front of him and scoots forward to lean back so he can rest his head on the sofa cushion.

"I could sleep some more. I was having a really good dream, too," he says.

"What was it about?" asks Allie. She often has good dreams where she is flying above cities and countryside; she can land anytime; she can hover above people and eavesdrop; she can turn to the left or to the right.

"We were in Savannah," says Richard, "We were at Mark's house. In fact, we were at a party," Richard laughs, "imagine that. Anyway, this Persian Cat came into the room and began talking."

"What color was the cat?" asks Allie.

"White, I think - maybe not -I don't remember, but the cat came into the room and started hypnotizing everyone." Richard yawns.

"Oh, that's funny," says Allie.

Richard continues, "The cat started telling everyone how to invest in the stock market to make a ton of money; then, while the cat was talking, everyone started jumping up and running around trying to find pencils and paper to write down things the cat said. I mean, this cat was giving some damned explicit tips."

"That's crazy!" Allie laughs.

Richard looks up at the porch ceiling, "I don't remember specific tips. Wish I did; sometimes in dreams there is psychic knowledge, you know, like how to play the lottery and win, stuff like that." He looks out onto the street, "What a sweet deal that would be."

"Naw," says Allie. "That would be too easy."

"No joke, I once knew a guy who dreamed about the numbers '6' and '7'. He went to the horse races and placed his bet on horses 6 and 7 to win. They won! Made a ton of money, that guy." Richard yawns.

He picks up his coffee cup with both hands and holds it over his chest while he continues to lie back, clearly still tired, and continues, "I cannot honestly say I remember specifics from the dream. It just seems like nonsense to me now; just an odd dream that made me feel like I was in control of something for a few seconds."

"Today's the 5th," says Allie, "It's Saturday. Do you want to go back to Atlanta today or tomorrow?"

Richard's eyes are tired; Allie can see it. He had, maybe, too much of a good time last night. She remembers seeing him, at some point in the evening, in a line dance going down the center of the line beside a rather handsome blonde slender male who had slung his coat over his shoulder and who slithered down the line, his white shirt partially un-tucked from his pants.

"Well, I still need to find a piece of furniture for a client. I've looked all over Atlanta and can't find anything that's right. Let's go shopping here today; we can go back tomorrow," he says. "Yeah, tomorrow, Sunday, we can go back then – get a good night's sleep; get up early, no traffic. Let's do it that way."

"Fine with me," says Allie.

Later, they drive across the bridge to the Island, have a shrimp burger, make the usual art gallery stops; they pull up in front of the Vintage Antique Mall. "I've always had good luck in here," says Richard. "Let's go in."

"Rock Around The Clock" plays on the canned music inside the store. Set up in individual booths, most which are interestingly decorated, prices vary widely from booth to booth. Vintage stores, which used to be fun, have oddly become more painful to experience. Thoughts give way to 'I remember Aunt Selma used this every Christmas to make Gingerbread Cookies. The best part of the cookie was the icing.' Or, 'Uncle Jack brought back a pillow from the war just like this one; wonder whatever happened to it?' Or, 'My sister and I always fought over who got to use the Easy Bake Oven. These days some lawyer would find a way to extract money from the Easy Bake Oven Enterprises for one hazard or another.' Faster than a rising muffin, the company would be bankrupt.

Richard flips around a price tag on a bamboo birdcage, "So, tell me more about your third husband; what's his name?"

Allie laughs, "I'm not telling you a thing! And, no more talk about what you obviously regard as nonsense."

"Why do you say that?" Richard raises an eyebrow.

"These days, I'm not too sure of anything," says Allie.

"Oh, I see," says Richard, "so, no proposal, I gather." He narrows his lips, obviously being teasingly mean, as he surveys a set of platters with quail on them, "Look at these," he says, "I have the matching teapot; I really ought to buy these." But, he sits them back down and continues to walk.

Allie opens up a little, "The thing about this guy is that I keep running into him when I'm out and about."

"Maybe he is a stalker," says Richard.

"Oh, come on, Richard. Don't be so funny; I think there is such a thing as destiny. Don't you?"

"Heck, no," he says, "I think you just travel in the same circles; that's all."

"Maybe we do," says Allie. End of conversation, she decides;

why had she even opened up to him in the first place? She presses her lips shut with two fingers, a subliminal gesture to herself that she would say no more on the subject.

Richard finds a round game table in the back of the store. It has a pedestal base cut from a tree trunk, and has four curved drawers the circle of the circumference of the table. The pulls are branch-shaped brass pulls.

"Look at that!" he says, in his most enthusiastic voice all weekend, "How unusual."

In depth, he examines the drawers; bends down to look more closely at the pedestal and how it is attached to the table. He runs his hand over the finish and peers more closely at the top, taking off his glasses to look very closely for nicks and indentions on the top of the table.

"This is an example of something that could have been made by an artist," he says, enthusiastically. "This might be a one-of-a-kind piece. Stuff like this can be very valuable."

Allie looks more closely at the table. It is interesting: rustic in design, carefully crafted. She wonders, though, if it truly is of value why does it sit here in back of an old dusty antique mall? Who quit loving their table? Did children of the deceased liquidate an entire estate, not wanting to be bothered with relics or ashes of lives long past?

"If you think it is what your client is looking for, I'd say get it," she says.

"I'd say, you're right; sold!" Richard pulls the tag off the table and starts toward the front of the store to pay. No quail platters today. The one-of-a-kind tree branch table, whose destiny becomes to grace a new home, is the star of today.

CHAPTER

Eight o'clock on a Monday, after having been absent from work a full ten days, it is Allie's plan to go to work. Is it possible that, given the summer season, no one will have noticed she has been absent? If something is said, might not she say: 'Are you sure it was 10 days? I think it was only about 3 or 4; probably felt like 10 days to you.' Still, it becomes increasingly obvious that soon something must be done about this boring existence called gainful employment.

Allie walks into the office, turning her head toward the wall, in an effort to avoid human contact. Someone calls out to her, "Good Morning." She calls out an automatic 'good morning' with eyes straight ahead, while she makes her way to the back of the office to the safety of the coffee station. During the walk, she passes rows and rows of individual cubicles – some are decorated with green frogs and sunshine flowers; some are as blank and vacant as the Northside Marta Station.

About to reach the decaf coffee pot unscathed, she sees out of the corner of her eye a couple who stand by the pot, sipping coffee and chatting. She doesn't recognize them, but, just in case, she pretends to be snapping shut her purse so she can at least pretend she is so involved with her purse that she doesn't see them. It is too late for that, however, as one of them calls out, "Did you have a nice 4th?"

Allie doesn't look up, but engages in automatic, autopilot-type conversation: "Yes, it was very restful."

"That's the idea, huh," says the person.

Allie walks to the coffee urn and busies herself with the ceremony of coffee, adding two sugars, some creamer, and a dash of cinnamon; stir, taste, more cream; stir again; dispose of trash; wipe counter with napkin; tuck napkin around the cup and proceed to her cubicle.

"Did you go out of town?" the person persists.

"Uh, no," Allie walks faster toward the front of the office. She will walk over to the floor-to-ceiling wall of windows and scan the sky for rain. There maybe she can stand and peacefully sip coffee.

Atlanta is filling up fast. Development is claiming grass and trees, yet no one seems to notice. All up and down Peachtree Street and Roswell Road, single one-story houses have been leveled and turned into massive multi-use concoctions chokingly crammed with clothing stores, restaurants, spas, grocery stores, gyms and apartments for rent. These new structures obscure trees, and chase away squirrels, deer, and little red foxes, who must now find a home as far away as Duluth and Suwanee. Banks look like mausoleums, and previous farm land, now paved over in straight lines and decorated to look like cookie-cutter movie sets, becomes the new Phoenix rising from cow paths.

On the street below, two pedestrians look like specks wearing clothing. They walk to the corner, press the button, and wait patiently for relentless traffic that speeds, screeches, turns left, runs red lights. Then, the pedestrians cross the street staying within newly painted white lines, running slightly as they cross. Yellow warning tripods, informing motorists that to hit a pedestrian is punishable by law, sit squarely between white lines, yet go largely ignored. All over town there are daily reports of people being struck by cars; maybe the signs need to be larger.

"Allie," a man calls. Allie turns around to face her boss, "Good to see you," he says.

"Thanks," she says, and she takes a sip of coffee.

"Did you have a nice 4th?" he asks.

"The best," she says. She hopes he was gone the entire 10 days and never noticed that she was also.

"Seems like forever since I've seen you," he hands her a sheet of paper with numbered bullets trailing all down the page. "Here are your assignments for today. It is quite long – understandable after time off. Just do what you can," he says.

She takes the paper and feels a wave of relief; she should have worried about nothing. Everything has returned to normal; nothing changes; days drone on; sameness equals comfort. She is surprised at her reaction, "Thanks," she says.

Her boss walks away from the window. Allie sees a shadow fall to the right of her, and she hears a man's voice, "I have been trying to get your attention all morning."

Allie raises her head for the first time today. "Dan! I'm sorry. Were you talking to me earlier?" she asks.

"Yeah," he says. "First, I said good morning."

"I know," she says

"Then I asked you about your 4th," he continues.

"I know," she says, "sorry."

"Preoccupied?" he asks.

"Probably," she says.

"Preoccupied with something worthwhile, I hope," he smiles.

"Oh, just the usual, Dan: friends, the beach house, the job."

Dan laughs. He shakes his head, blows an exaggerated breath out of the corner of his mouth; she sips the coffee.

"I hear you," he says.

"So, what's up?" she asks.

"Well, today several of us are going to take a long lunch; why don't you join us?" he asks.

"A long lunch as in – still celebrating the 4th?" she asks.

"Not really. It's someone's birthday and we want to go to Kobe Steaks on Roswell Road," he says.

"Oh, you can definitely count me in on that," she says. "I don't think I have had a decent meal in" - she counts the days she has been gone from work – "in maybe 10 days."

"Ten days," says Dan, "Poor baby. Okay, we'll swing by your desk and pick you up when we're ready to go."

"Great," she says. She remembers the last time she went to Kobe Steaks. She had been starving that day. The Asian chef had walked out, and after washing the grill, poured half a dozen beaten eggs over the grill and began to chop, stir, and scramble. Next, he chopped up a bunch of other stuff and worked it into the eggs. Then, he worked everything into a big tub of white rice. She remembers how when the chef began to cut off shrimp tails, he tossed the tails into his tall chef hat, missing half of the time so that the shrimp tails landed on the floor. She had wondered if he was a new chef who hadn't learned the hat balancing act yet; or had he been simply clowning around?

CHAPTER
Eleven

It is Saturday morning and Allie has decided: today is the day to get a dog. Arriving at Petco early, she vows to remain sober and unemotional throughout the animal adoption process. First, she will calmly walk through the store and merely survey the landscape, looking at all the animals, cats as well as dogs. Then, she will determine which animal looks to be the healthiest. She will also try to determine which animal appears to have suffered the least amount of neurotic damage done by previous owners, and she will make the adoption decision accordingly.

Stopping first by the cat station, she sees three tiny, grey-striped kittens. One of them, upon seeing her, struggles to stand on his newborn feet. The kitten makes its way on unsteady paws to her side of the cage and presses a cold nose to Allie's finger. The other two siblings are fast asleep, wrapped around each other. Although they are insanely adorable, she doesn't even consider adopting one of them. They will have no trouble finding a good home; will be, no doubt, the first animals to go.

There are two more cats in cages. In one of the cages a large yellow cat hisses at her when she approaches. The other cage houses a calico who sees her and emits a loud meow. It walks toward the front of the cage where it stands and it looks at her. Allie can see one eye is swollen practically shut. An attendant in a blue apron walks over and speaks up, "He really needs a good home, that one."

"What's wrong with his eye?" asks Allie.

"Oh, he's a survivor, that one. He has had everything wrong with him," says the attendant. "We found him wandering along I-285. We call him our miracle cat; he is lucky to be alive. He is much stronger now because we have been feeding him Max Cat."

Allie can feel her emotional resolve begin to crumble, "What is Max Cat?" she asks.

"It's just a cat food," says the attendant, "really high in calories with lots of vitamins and things good for cats."

"Oh," Allie looks back at the cat, determined he is not the pet she will adopt.

"That little guy," the attendant continues, "was so skinny. He had worms, ringworm, and a severe eye infection from which he is recovering nicely. You should have seen him before; both eyes were swollen shut. He looked like an alien."

Allie backs away from the cage. "I actually came in specifically for a dog," she says. "I would like a little playmate to walk with in Piedmont Park."

"Okay, dogs are back there." The attendant points toward the back of the store.

Fully aware that sweat has begun to collect on the back of her neck, Allie walks briskly toward the large cages in the back of the store where three dogs wait to be adopted. The biggest dog looks like Lab and Shepard mix. His mouth is open as if to smile; his tongue hangs out and little drops of saliva fall from his tongue. When he sees Allie approach he jumps up and rests paws on the side of the cage. Allie eases her hand toward him to pat his head, "Good boy," she says.

"Oh," says a voice standing to the right of her, "He isn't a boy; he is a 'she'."

Allie looks up at the man who has just spoken to her and her heart drops. It is him! They keep bumping into one another! Maybe Richard was right; maybe this man really is a stalker.

"I cannot believe this!" he says.

"I know; me neither," Allie smiles.

"We must definitely be on the same schedule," he says returning the smile. "I think it is time," he says as he extends his hand to Allie, "that I introduce myself to you." He takes her hand in his, and all Allie can think of is how she once read in an Amy Vanderbilt Etiquette Book that a woman should be first to extend her hand to a man. But, she takes his hand and shakes it as he continues, "My name is Jim." Touching his hand gives her a zing that could be static electricity, or it could be sheer chemistry. "Jim Lunden," he adds.

"My name is Allie," she says.

"Good to finally put a name to such a beautiful face," he says.

"Why, thank you," says Allie.

An awkward moment passes between them and they both turn back to face the dog cage. Jim is first to break the silence.

"How have you been?" he asks.

"I've been good," says Allie; "You?"

"The same," he says. "Making the rounds, you know. Squeezing in a little work between junk stores," he laughs.

"Yeah, me too," she says.

"Found any good stuff lately?" he asks.

"Well, actually, yes," she says.

He looks at her, eyebrows wide, open to an intricate description of the latest unearthed treasure.

"I was at an antique store in Savannah with a friend of mine who is an Interior Designer and we found a rustic table that was made, possibly by an artist," she says.

"H-m-m-m," he says. His eyes filter a question which causes Allie to wonder if Jim would, indeed, consider the table Richard bought to be a 'find.'

"What things do you typically look for when you go junking?" she asks.

Tools mostly," he says, "Things I can use in the business."

"In your business?" she asks. "What business?"

"I have the repair shop right there on Peachtree by Oglethorpe University," he says.

"You're kidding!" says Allie. "I know it well; have passed it a million times: Lunden's Repairs. I go by it every day on my way to work, in fact!" she says.

"Do you?" He seems genuinely surprised. "Where do you work?"

"I'm in one of those high-rise office buildings right off 14th Street and Peachtree," she says.

"You know, Allie," Jim looks over at dog food snacks that sit in even rows on shelves, "We should go out sometime."

"That would be fun," says Allie.

"Here," he produces a piece of paper and a pen and hands it to her. "Write down your number and I'll call you in a couple of days."

Allie does as she is told, marveling at how easily this has happened, yet, not really all that easy. Ten years the two of them have been bumping into one another. Obviously, they travel in the same small circle. She looks more closely at him when she hands back the piece of paper. He wears a cap and t-shirt. A full head of curly gray hair peeks out from under the cap. He is quite a bit taller than she; not fat. He has big fingers – worker's fingers. He is handsome; a dimple lines his cheek; a light belly begins to form above the belt like most middle-aged men. But, overall, he is trim; his hands are smooth; fingernails clean. And, when he smiles, there is a twinkle.

CHAPTER

True to his word, Jim calls the second day and they agree upon a time to meet the following Friday. He will pick her up at 7:00 p.m. and they will go out to dinner.

When he arrives at the condo Friday night, Allie shows him around. He likes the color of paint on the walls. He comments about how large the rooms are. He stands in front of her fireplace and admires an oil painting that Allie painted 15 years ago when life was simple enough so as to allow time to paint. The painting, a scene of two ships resting in the harbor, seems to trigger something in Jim, and he turns to Allie, "We have a lot in common," he says.

"Do you paint too?" asks Allie.

"No," he says, "I play music."

So here it is: a fairy tale threatening to come true. Standing before Allie, the dreamer, is Jim, handsome businessman, renaissance man, music man, who has admired her from afar for 10 years.

Their date is fun; he confesses he has 'had his eye on her' for a long time. Allie tries to act as if she would never suspect this. He discusses a marriage that happened and ended during this 10-year timeframe. Allie discovers he is a few years younger than her, which is no surprise. She learns that he likes 'mature' women, which is quite a surprise.

On every journey, there exists a brief moment, maybe only a second, maybe for 15 minutes, where the traveler has to decide in which direction to turn, because the traveler can easily go in either direction. The person about to embark has two notions about the direction in which he should take. One notion is a logical direction; the other is a wild card direction, solely influenced by the heart. Dreamers usually follow the heart.

Jim talks about music and his experiences while playing music in a band on the road. Allie listens and looks at his profile. There is the dimple, the evenly formed lips, the navy blue eyes, the slightly Roman hook to the nose. There is a young, fun spirit and a reserved, kind gentleness that influences his looks and turns him into a handsome and solid new romance. Alas, the journey begins.

After dinner, he takes her home and he walks into the condo with her. While they stand just inside the door, she says she had fun. Jim looks at Allie and asks, "Do you mind if I have a hug?"

"Sure." She pushes her arms up under his and he pulls her close. His arms around her neck, her arms crisscrossed over his back, he says, "I have been waiting a long time for this."

After the hug, he moves toward the door, saying, hand on doorknob, "I'll call you tomorrow."

This drama, simple and quite ordinary, unfolding on its own, was neither planned nor expected. One day Allie, coasting through a humdrum life, now happens upon a completely different path.

As soon as the door closes, the phone rings and without missing a beat, she picks it up. "H-e-l-l-o, Allie; this is Elyquia," says the happy voice. "How are you?"

"I'm good," says Allie. She almost tells Elyquia about her date with Jim, but decides against it just in case things don't work out. At the same time, she makes a mental note to discuss it no more with Richard, either.

"How are you doing? How's your guy?" Allie asks Elyquia.

"Oh," Elyquia laughs in gusts, "he is g-r-e-a-t!" She says 'great' the way a smiling person would say 'great.' Once Allie had a telemarketing job that suggested you smile into the phone while talking to prospective customers. The telemarketing boss would march up and down the rows between cubicles, tie askew on a rumpled white shirt, holding two index fingers either side of his mouth in an exaggerated smile as a reminder to smile.

"Has he asked you out again?" asks Allie.

"Oh, yes," says Elyquia. "Things are heating up," she says. "That's why I am thinking we should start up our little business pretty soon so he will think we started it before we met."

Their little business: the women had once dreamed up a money-making brainstorm which would capitalize on their free time and their sense of fun. The business would be named TWO DATING DIVAS. It would cater to men who needed a date: still unmarried men trying to get anxious mothers off their backs, men who needed to impress either a boss who made it a requirement that their employees were married, or any man who just needed to present themselves as being on a date. The women would pose as their dates or pose as their wives, where, calling upon acting skills, would act fond of the guy; they would straighten his tie while looking lovingly at his profile; they would slip in 'honey' once in a while. They would charge $150 a date; have a nice dinner and go home.

Now, however, the business doesn't seem like such a good idea. What if she happened to be on a 'date' and ran into Jim?

Allie struggles between full disclosure versus smoke and mirrors. "Elyquia," she says, finally. "Let me think about it a little more. Right now might not be a good time."

Elyquia surprises her with her answer, "I know what you mean," she says, simply.

"We'll talk more about it later," says Allie.

"Okay, Sweetie; get a good night's rest," says Elyquia. "I'll talk to you tomorrow."

Allie hangs up the phone and walks out onto the patio. The night air is cooler; August is moving in. Soon it will be September; then will come the holidays: November, Turkey, December with red and green everywhere. This Christmas might be different than last; there might be some celebrating going on.

A rising evening wind blows onto the patio and moves the straw roman shades that hang in the windows: night air that smells like it comes directly off the water of the French Riviera. She shuts the patio door and goes to bed.

CHAPTER
Thirteen

On their second date, Jim and Allie go to a bar and restaurant in the suburbs, a 45-minute drive from Atlanta where he sometimes plays in a band. Quite musically accomplished, he can either play the bass guitar as well as 12-string, acoustic or electric guitar, and is often asked at the last minute to jam with other musicians.

Near dusk, they pull into the crowded parking lot of Mac's Big Daddy Bar. The outside patio, filled to near capacity, flickers under overhead lights in colors pink and blue. From inside loud music files through heavy leaded glass doors that open to the restaurant foyer.

Jim opens the trunk of his Mercedes, reaches for a black bag and hands it to Allie, "Carry this for me, will you?"

"Sure," she says. "Am I your roadie tonight?"

He laughs and hands her a folded guitar stand, "Take this too," he grins.

"That's a yes, I guess," she says.

"That's definitely a yes. You can be my roadie any day of the week." He drops down the car trunk door, picks up two black guitar cases, and the two of them walk toward the club. Filing past couples on the patio, curious voyeurs who watch as the musician and the roadie make their way past,

Jim reaches the foyer first and holds open the heavy door for Allie, setting down one of the guitar cases to do so.

Once inside, he walks straight toward the stage where a small band is set up and already playing. The drummer, hat on backwards, waves drumsticks over the drums. A bald-headed guitar player plays free style on a shiny red guitar, adding improvised flourishes to the strings; he smiles broadly when he sees Jim.

Once the song ends, Jim takes Allie's hand and leads her to the stage where he introduces her to Elliott, host of the show, and to the guitarist and to the drummer. She sees a stack of CDs sitting on a music stand in front of Elliott, and a tip jar sits in front of that. To the left of the tip jar sits a glass of liquid with ice and a lemon slice in it.

Elliot takes Allie's hand and gives it a brief shake, "Nice to meet you," he says. "Have you heard Jim play yet?" he asks.

Allie shakes her head, "Nope. I'm looking forward to it, though."

"He's good," Elliott says simply.

Taking a seat at a table near the band, Allie looks at the swarm of people in the bar. She turns back and watches Jim open one of the guitar cases, set the guitar in the stand, then open the other case and hoist the guitar up, tossing the red strap around his neck. He clips a capo to the neck of the guitar, closes the case and stashes it beside the drummer.

Stepping briefly off the stage, Jim walks over and motions towards a nearby table, "Why don't you move closer?" he says. "There will be more people in soon – the other groupies - and they'll sit here with you," he winks and turns to walk back to the stage, as the music starts up again.

Once back onstage, Jim bends over a black box and fiddles with the knobs. A couple of people walk through the door, and Elliott makes eye contact, smiles and points toward the table where Allie sits. A tall redhead with a permanent half-smile on her face sits down and introduces herself to Allie by extending her hand, "I'm Cherry," she says.

Taking her hand for a brief informal half-shake, Allie says, "I'm Allie; pleased to meet you."

"Who are you here with?" asks Cherry, as she watches her man walk up onto the stage, his hair standing straight up, which looks like a grown-out flat top.

Allie points to Jim, "I'm with him."

"Great guitarist," Cherry's half smile remains unchanged, as if her real thoughts are ten miles away somewhere else. She turns around, flags the waitress, and orders chicken wings and a rum and Coke. "Have you ordered yet?" she asks Allie.

"No, we just got here, actually," says Allie.

"Oh?" Cherry turns around again and yells to the waitress, "Bring us menus, will ya?"

The waitress, who wears a stern expression that indicates being busy more than anything else, very efficiently produces a menu and lays it on the table. Raising her eyebrows, she looks at Allie and asks, "What can I get ya?"

Glancing at the unopened menu in her hands, Allie says, "Let me start with a Diet Coke."

"You got it," says the waitress, who walks away as quickly as she had appeared.

While the band plays Drops of Jupiter, Allie sneaks a peek at the crowd: a middle-aged, after-work assortment of people with a couple of young girls who sit at the bar, their long hair trailing straight down slim backs. One bald-headed man with a hoop earring in one ear hangs over one of the girls, who probably thinks he adores her, while he probably thinks he is going to get lucky.

Looking back at the band, Allie surmises now might be a good time to more closely observe Jim while he is thoroughly engrossed in what he is doing. From time to time he turns to the drummer and plays toward him, then he turns back to Elliott; there is no mistaking he is having a good time. The crowd is also having fun, with several couples getting up to dance, one girl with long straight blonde hair peeking out from under a man's Fedora, dances by herself and is joined from time to time by other single women who dance for a while then sit back down.

A new couple, who walk in and wave to Cherry, pull up stools to the table and sit, placing a purse and a shopping bag on hooks along the wall behind the table. The man, 40-ish and attractive, already seems to know Allie because when she is introduced by Cherry he says to her, "You must be the girl Jim has been talking about." He reaches an arm around the waist of the girl with him, "This is my date, Judy."

Looking friendly and open, Judy smiles and says, "Hi, nice to meet you." Then she leans very close to Allie and whispers, "Jim invited Harrison and me to meet the 'new girl he really liked.'" To punctuate what she has just said, Judy points two fingers at Allie and laughs, "That would be you!"

Instantly, Allie feels a kinship with Judy, as if they have been friends for centuries, "Is that what Jim said?" she asks.

Judy brings the two fingers to her chest, "Cross my heart," she says.

Allie watches Jim while he plays. Engrossed in the song, he is oblivious now to any crowd around him. Two women have danced in front of Elliott, and one of them stops to say something to him while the other one drops money into the tip jar. In answer to her comment, Elliott says, "As long as you two continue to dance with each other I will. I LIVE to see women dance together." He says this with no shortage of cynicism, and Allie thinks it odd how she can hear stage conversation above the music and the crowd.

Looking behind her, Judy spots an empty table and turns back to Allie, "Why don't we scoot these tables together. There will be more people coming."

"Sure." Allie hops up and helps Judy push the tables together. The band, now in full swing mode, plays "Mustang Sally" and Allie resists dancing in place or joining other women on the dance floor, one of whom, a bit tipsy, raises her hands above her head and sings: "All you wanna do is ride around Sally. Ride Sally ride."

The song brings back memories. Pregnant with her son, Allie and husband Sean once drove across the Texas panhandle on their way to Amarillo in Sean's green GTO. Because of her pregnancy and after stopping several times to pee, Sean had jokingly announced, 'You sure are a lot of trouble.' But, he had said it with affection; he had smiled; he stopped many times – as many times as it took to make it to Amarillo. The marriage seems so far in the background as to appear more like a dream than an actuality. Why had it ended? Now, she remembers only the good times; how he had thought her dimples were where the angels kissed her. Even when they had divorced he still loved her, he said.

Harrison leans across the table in Allie's direction and calls to her, "How are things going with you and Jim?"

"So far so good," she says, being purposefully non-committal.

Harrison leans back, obviously satisfied with that response, and by this time the waitress has arrived to take orders, so he orders Nachos; Allie orders the Pecan Orange Salad; Judy says she will order later.

Cherry pushes her plate of Chicken Wings toward Judy, "Have one," she says.

Judy takes a wing and says, "Thank you." Cherry pushes the plate toward Allie, "Eat the rest," she says.

"Actually, I just ordered," says Allie, but she takes a wing anyway and presses it to her lips. It is hot with lots of red pepper; hot wings – staple food of the South. The pepper burns her lips while a delicious taste of hot vinegary juice burns her tongue. As she bites into the wing, she looks at Jim. He winks and the music plays: "This is for all the single people; thinking that love has passed them by. Don't give up until you drink from the silver cup; you never know until you try."

CHAPTER

Sitting on the patio holding a cup of steaming green tea, Allie looks out past the cars in the parking lot, to the trees on the hill. Once going into September, it will be too chilly to wear the strapless ball gown that she once bought at a vintage store, so she has decided to surprise Jim on their next date and wear the gown even though it might feel awkward. She might feel conspicuous - who wears ball gowns these days, anyway? Maybe the Real Housewives of Somewhere Else wear ball gowns. Wealthy Atlanta debutantes wear ball gowns; senior prom goers wear ball gowns, but middle-aged women?

Maybe she should give Jim advance notice of the intent to wear the ball gown; be perfectly certain as not to overdress for the occasion. Or, no, maybe she should simply answer the door wearing the gown, because the ideal occasion has come up to wear the gown, as Jim informed her he has tickets to the Fox Theatre for the Jackson Browne concert happening in exactly two days. When he told her that, she hinted that she might dress up for the concert, especially since it is going to be at the Fox Theatre. On second thought, maybe she will just answer the door wearing the gown, or maybe she will show up at his house wearing it.

Allie sets the cup of tea down on the table and goes inside and pulls the ball gown from the closet and tries it on. It is pretty obvious why no one had previously purchased this beautiful copper-colored strapless dream; it is so small in the waist she almost has trouble zipping it. For a moment, she thinks she might have to go next door and ask Millie to help her zip up the dress. Maybe she won't wear it after all.

Soon the zipper slips past the tight spot, the dress is on and Allie faces the mirror. The vision is stunning. Her hair, copper colored as well, falls almost to her collarbone. Below the hair, there is a wide space of pale skin before the dress takes over and continues the copper color all the way to the floor. The material, of crinoline weight, falls beautifully and rustles when she turns. Briefly, she considers that this full-length strapless gown might actually be too dressy for any occasion in Atlanta that she would ever attend. She thinks of the one person who would know the answer to the question, and goes to the phone to dial Richard's number.

"Hello," Richard answers on the second ring. He is always on the phone; he loves to talk on the phone, and often his phone will have a busy signal for hours on end.

"Richard," she says.

"Hey, Allie, what's up?" he says.

"I need another favor," she says.

"Oh, god," he says, but Allie knows he lives to cater to people.

"No, no, it's good," she says, "You will like this project."

He perks up a bit, "Okay, shoot," he says.

"I need some fashion advice," she says.

"Such as," he says.

"I need you to look at this dress that I am considering wearing on my next date and tell me if it is too dressy for the occasion," she says.

"A date, huh?" he says, "Would this be a date with your next husband?"

"Cute, Richard, cute," says Allie. Soon she will have to tell him all about Jim; how they met, on and on.

"You're right, good taste is my forte," his voice brightens. "What'cha doing right now?" he asks.

"Trying on the dress," she says, "Can you come over?"

"Of course, let me finish up with some stuff. I'll be right over," he hangs up the phone.

Not more than fifteen minutes later, Richard knocks on Allie's door and she answers it wearing the dress. Richard breezes into the room, purses his lips, and lets out a puff of air that has no sound. Then he takes a deep breath.

"You're right," he says, then grimaces, "That is a pretty formal dress."

"I know," she says.

"Don't get me wrong," he says, "It is a beautiful dress. Where are you going?" he asks. Allie can tell he is getting excited by the way he does in a fabric store when he finds a fabric that matches a rug that goes with a lamp that he found at some estate sale for $9.99.

"To a concert," she says.

Obviously, Richard is much more curious about the concert than about what to do with the dress because he raises an eyebrow, waiting for her to expound, but he soon recovers. "Yeah, it's a little dressy. Maybe you could wear it to the Opera," he says.

"Richard," says Allie, "When am I ever going to go to the opera?"

"You never know," he says, with a straight face, "that third husband of yours might very well take you to the opera one day."

"Oh, good lord!" Allie says.

He walks toward her and picks up the hem of the dress. "People in Atlanta don't really dress up to go to a concert, you know," he says. He drops the hem; it falls back down to the floor; he scoots away to survey the scene from afar.

"You're right," says Allie, "So you are saying it is definitely too dressy?"

Richard bends down, picks up the hem again and tucks it up under the dress so that it falls just below Allie's knee.

"Well, wait a minute," he says. "Why don't you hem it up to here?" he pushes the dress around into various configurations until it yields a poofy-looking hemline.

"That's it!" he says. "Hem it at intervals and it will be really blousy at the bottom. Very in style," he says, waving his hands in the air, as it is obvious he is now getting more excited.

"Let's try it," says Allie. "Have a seat on the sofa. I'm going into the bedroom and take it off and pin it up."

Richard seems surprised, "You're going to do it right now?"

"I'm only going to go into the bedroom and pin it up. I'll be right back. Help yourself to a Coke in the fridge." She walks down the hall toward the bedroom.

"Hey," Richard calls from behind her, "Tell me more about this date. Who are you going with, seriously."

Allie goes into the bedroom, removes the dress and tucks it up all around. She positions the tucks at evenly spaced intervals, securing them with safety pins. When the hem is completely pinned up all around, she puts the dress back on and looks at it in the mirror. It falls just below the knee and flares at the bottom just like a balloon-bottomed hemline.

She walks back into the front room to find Richard seated in the chair nearest the door. He smiles when he sees her, "That's perfect!" he says. He throws back his head and shakes his fists at the ceiling, "Oh, god, now I'm a dress designer!"

"Thanks for your help," says Allie, "I feel better in the dress. Full length is just too formal these days, isn't it?"

"Yes, for most things, yes; now, tell me more," he persists,

"Who is your date? It's time; come clean. I thought you were just joking at first; now I can see you are serious."

"Richard, I promise you we'll talk about it someday."

Richard rolls his eyes; shrugs, "What did I expect?" he says.

This will be the fourth date with Jim. He picks her up at home and when he brings her back, they sit on the patio and talk. On their last date, however, they graduated inside and sat on the sofa, where they had talked more at length about their lives. That night he said maybe next time Allie should come over and see his place.

"Richard, thanks so much for your help," says Allie.

"Of course," he says.

"You may very well be my best friend," she says.

"Yeah," he says, "I know."

"Also, I want you to know that I appreciate all those trips to the beach you took with me," she says, "when I was..."

"AFRAID to drive," Richard interrupts.

"Not afraid to drive," says Allie, "Just afraid."

"I know; AFRAID!" he says, "I'm glad you're admitting it; afraid to live."

"Everyone's afraid, Richard," she says.

"I know. That's what drugs are for," he says.

"Bob had just died," she defends herself.

"I know; I know," he says, "Just relax. I'm kidding – sort of."

"Thanks anyway," she says.

"Shut up," he says.

CHAPTER

Fifteen

It turns out, as is often the case in fairytales, that Allie awakens the morning after the concert in Jim's bed, his arms still around her and the ball gown lying on the floor alongside the side of the bed. She turns her head to watch, while he is sleeping, the off-guard, vulnerable way, mouth slightly open, that he breathes through open lips. At the window, the roman shades belie light behind them, but sun filters through the sides of the shades indicating that it is late in the morning; it might even be noon. Looking at the ceiling, she relives the date, in a word: magical. They had waited above the theatre in the open-air lounge, having drinks before the concert. Although the crowd had been dressed in various styles, most everyone had been, to some extent, formally dressed. Nevertheless, heads had turned when Allie and Jim made their way into the lounge all the way to the back where finally they found a couple willing to share their sofa while they also waited for the concert to begin.

The couple, over from Macon, owned a trucking company. The wife complained how her husband never dressed in anything but jeans, but that tonight she had made him dress up. She worked for the college, she said. She also loved Jackson Browne; her sister had wanted to come, but decided at the last moment to stay home because she was recovering from a broken heart and was afraid the sad songs of Jackson Browne would just make her cry.

There was an agreeable joy visiting with a couple that Allie and Jim would probably never see again, trading casual pleasantries not destined for any agenda. It had been kind of them to share their sofa on the crowded outdoor rooftop, but soon the concert would start, so they said their farewells, actually walked into the Fox Theatre together where they were soon separated by the throngs of people struggling to take seats before the concert began.

After the concert, Allie and Jim had gone to an all-night diner; had gone back to his house where he lit a candle, set the candle down on the nightstand, and motioned to her with both hands.

Scarcely able to resist kissing Jim's open, sleeping mouth, she does so, then whispers in his ear, "I think I am going to go on home."

He opens his eyes a bit; sees her and pulls her tightly to him, where she returns the embrace, and they stay tightly together for a long minute. Releasing the embrace, he says, "I'll get up with you."

He sits up on the bed, walks to the closet and pulls out a black and grey checked robe, and while he is tying the robe, he watches Allie put on the ball gown. Coming around to her side of the bed, he helps bring the zipper up past her waist. "You looked so beautiful last night," he says.

"Thank you," she turns around and puts her arms around his neck, having to reach up to do so because without her heels, she is quite a bit shorter than he.

"In fact," he says, "you are beautiful, period."

"Thank you," she says, smiling up at his eyes.

"Inside and out," he continues.

"Thank you again," she says. He takes her hand; together they walk into the kitchen where she will exit the house by the side door – exactly the way they had come in last night.

Once they get to the door, he says, hand on doorknob, "Drive carefully."

"I will," she says. He opens the door and together they peer outside. "It's going to be a beautiful day," he says. "I'll call you later."

"Okay," says Allie, and she steps out the door onto the first step, but Jim still has hold of her hand.

"Wait," he says. He pulls her back inside and once more puts his arms around her, "Last night was a blast. I had fun," he says.

"Yeah, me too," says Allie.

Taking her hand, he kisses her again and says once more, "I'll call you later."

When Allie gets in her car, she sees that she had forgotten to deposit checks in the bank so she decides after checking the time, that she still has a short window of time to do so before the banks close; she'll run by, deposit the checks and then go home.

Driving past strip mall stores and coffee shops in this unfamiliar neighborhood, making her way across town to her bank, she plays over and over in her head scenes from last night's date. She had not been prepared for how easy and comfortable everything had been.

Arriving at the bank, she is tempted to use the drive-through window because she is wearing the ball gown, but, suddenly, seized by a devilish temptation to have some fun with her own recreated version of Breakfast At Tiffany's where Audrey Hepburn gets out of a limo early in the morning in front of Tiffany's and stands window shopping while wearing a full-length black and white gown, eating a doughnut out of a white paper bag, Allie opts at the last minute to park the car and go inside the bank where she will act as if there is nothing unusual about a woman wearing a copper colored ball gown while making a $500 deposit.

She walks up to the door of the bank and looks in. There are about five people standing in line, but the line is moving fast, so, deposit in hand, she opens the door to the bank, approaches the line and is greeted by a woman sitting at a side desk. "Welcome to Suntrust," calls out the woman.

"Good morning," Allie says to her. The woman looks a tad puzzled, reaches her hand down beside her as if she might be ready to push a buzzer indicating there is a robbery taking place in the Suntrust Bank in the late morning on a beautiful, sunny Saturday.

Allie gets in line. A man standing at the teller window turns around, clears his throat, and smiles. She fiddles in her purse as if she is looking for something, which gives her the opportunity to look down and not make eye contact. Suddenly, she has begun to question her previously felt bravery to show up in broad daylight, in such a conservative establishment as a bank, wearing a strapless, puffy-at-the-hem ballgown.

Feeling the lip gloss come to hand, she, without a second thought, pulls it out, removes the top and sweeps raspberry lip gloss across her lips. No sooner has she done this than the young dark-haired male teller smiles and says, "I'll help the next person in line."

She walks to his window where, by now, the entire staff and bank full of customers are looking at her with affront-tinged curiosity. The young teller, however, perfectly unaffected and obviously schooled in impeccable customer service, smiles and says, "How are you today?"

Allie smiles at him, "Fine; and you?"

"Fine," he says.

She offers him the deposit, watching it slide across the cold marble counter, only looking up when he says, "O-o-o, I love your lipstick."

"Why, thank you," she says, surprised.

"I used to sell cosmetics," he says, "and I've seen some beautiful lip glosses, but that color is just gorgeous!"

"Thank you so much," says Allie. "Where did you work when you sold makeup?" she asks.

Not missing a beat, free spirits in this world of banking, the two continue their airy banter, "At Ulta for a while; then at Sephora."

Customers have formed a line behind her; she can hear throat-clearing.

"Oh, Sephora!" she continues, "that's my favorite store!"

"It was mine too," he says. "You can find everything there," she says.

"Yeah, I know. I miss it; I really do," he says with a pensive grin.

"I can see how you would." Allie glances sideways to the line beside her and sees that a woman with short salt and pepper- colored hair is staring her down with a slightly disdainful look. Allie smiles at the woman; continues her conversation with the teller, "The only problem with Sephora is that I buy too much when I'm there."

The teller laughs, "That's the idea, girl," he says.

Allie winks at him, instant friend, and takes her receipt. "Thank you for banking with SunTrust," he says.

"Thank you," she says. Turning around, headed toward the door, she notes the line, having grown behind her, consists of people, some of whom stare straight ahead, some of whom outwardly gawk, while she walks to the door, passing, once again, the seated lady at the desk, who repeats her initial greeting, "Thank you for banking with SunTrust."

Allie pushes open the bank door and walks past the ATM on her way to the car, where a guy standing at the ATM turns and watches her walk all the way to the car before he reaches out to get his money. She shuts the door of the car and begins the drive home. He probably thinks she is a hooker just coming from work.

CHAPTER
Sixteen

The morning air smells clean like soap. In the condo parking lot all the cars parked side by side, seem to sleep, their windows rolled up, some visor-protected from the scorching August sun that will rise later today. This morning's walk will be more comfortable because overnight rain has lowered the temperature.

Allie walks past secret burial grounds of soldiers past; walks past one unsuspecting house that sits silent and dark upon the ancient graveyard. She hears a distant barking dog that might be watching from an upstairs window.

She dreamed of dogs last night. The dream, so faint she can barely remember, contained several dogs that had come to her house for food; she had felt overwhelmed because for all the cans of sardines, soup, asparagus, and pears, there was not one whit of dog food anywhere in the house. What did the dream mean? Allie knows only one person who lives in a house with several dogs – her baby sister, Mandy.

Last year when Allie went home to visit her family, things at home had changed considerably. The topography that had been home was the same: more land than people, obese women shopping at Walmart pushing baskets piled high with food, handsome, rough-faced Midwestern Cowboys still attentive to attractive older women. That part of home was intact, yet chapters had begun to vary. Mandy, having come into an inheritance from the in-laws, had purchased a nice, new vehicle. Mandy, who seemed relaxed, no longer dependent, was finally coming into her own, for which Allie was grateful.

Mother had now enlisted a neighbor to drive her to the airport to pick up Allie, who still remembers being met at the airport by two elderly women, one hobbling more than Allie had remembered, the other one very brown and weather-beaten from working in her garden all summer long.

During that particular visit, Allie noticed her mother's guarded reaction to Mandy's newly found independence. She was suspicious of her obvious absence from some family interactions. She suspected there might be problems in her sister's marriage.

"What kind of problems?" Allie had asked.

"I don't know; maybe she's on drugs," Mother had said.

"Oh, Mother," Allie had said.

Her mother seemed more silent; she didn't pay much attention to Dad, who at 90 years of age had begun to lament how all his friends were dying and the only people to talk to were 'old people who talk about their gallbladder operations.' That last visit home had raised even more feelings of guilt at having literally deserted her entire family years ago, leaving them on the windy prairie, while she sought…what had she sought? There was no evidence of any gain; there seemed no answer to the question. The question had remained the plague.

Near the end of that particular visit, Allie's sister, Mandy, had expressed a desire to spend a day with Allie visiting the old home place about 15 miles down the road. The actual farmhouse, which had burned to the ground in the 1970s, consisted now of a mere cinder block foundation sitting atop a huge hole that had once been the basement. Accepting the invitation to be alone with her sister and to visit the old house where they had grown up, she had climbed into her sister's new vehicle, leaving Mom and Dad sitting under the shade tree in the front yard which Mother often referred to as "Dad's Office." Just before the door to the van was shut, Mom had risen from her chair under the tree, had walked to the door of the van and knocked on the window, "Do you want me to come with you girls?" she had asked.

Allie and Mandy had exchanged looks. The question had surprised them both, coming from a mother who might once have demanded, "I am coming with you!" but was now relegated to asking, "May I come?"

Mother's vulnerability had seemed new and out of place, but, surmising there must be a reason for Mandy's intent to be alone with her, Allie had acted as if Mom's quiet plea had not registered. Forcing a happy smile to her face and acting as if she had not heard Mother ask if she could come along, Allie had faked a cheerful wave goodbye, yet, in a last-minute attempt to ease the rebuff, she had rolled down the window and said something silly like, "When I get back, we'll make a nice salad with that lettuce in the garden."

Mother had slowly backed away from the vehicle and had sat down underneath the tree with her aging husband. She had waved goodbye, and as the girls drove away, Allie had felt regret grip her heart for the first time this visit home.

There was always a reason for tears, but this was the first time seeing aging parents was the cause of it.

The two sisters were down the country road only a few yards when Mandy had pulled over to the side of the road, checked the rear view mirror, and pulled out a fancy marijuana pipe. She produced an equally fancy butane lighter that looked more like a hand grenade than a lighter and she turned to Allie and said, "You are going to smoke pot with me, aren't you?"

Funny, Allie's son had prepared her for just this moment months earlier when he had called one morning with surprising revelations. "Mom," he had said, "You are so wrong about Grandma and Aunt Mandy. They do care about you; it's just that you are so different from them that you scare them. They don't hate you. They just don't know what to do with you."

It had become apparent to Allie that this outing with her sister was probably going to be some kind of epiphany; it might prove eye-opening at best. But, as they drove to the old home place, Mandy became more and more animated to the point that Allie began to wonder if there was something else in that pipe besides marijuana.

Allie could see why Mother had thought Mandy was on drugs because Mandy did seem more animated than usual, yet Allie sensed her sister was only seeking some sort of return to a lost freedom by returning to her childhood home. People who have lost their way often return home to find it again.

They had driven down the rocky road past newly erected

green street signs, which streets had recently been named after the farmers who had once settled the land. The first sign they passed said Christie Street. It had been named after the Christie family, a family of Cherokee Indians, blind from diabetes. They used to sit out on their front porch at night and play gospel music on electric guitars, sending beautiful music into evening air.

The next street, Velnik Street, was named after the hard-working German Velnik family famous for growing all their own vegetables, smoking all their own meat, cooking over a kerosene stove and pumping water from a natural well.

When Allie had seen MacKay Street she sat up straight in her seat. Their grandfather, Donald MacKay, would have been so proud to see a monument, in the form of a street named after him, to that section of land he once settled and wrestled with to turn brush to hay, to clear rocks for a rose garden, to raise cattle and to butcher them, to raise six children and then to die young. He would have been proud to see his name on a green street sign planted just aside the long winding road that led down to his old home place.

Allie had sat holding onto the hand strap above her head while they jostled their way down that bumpy country road. Mandy's mood had brightened the further into the country they drove, she who had always reacted the opposite to home than had Allie. In the country, Mandy acted free; Allie felt trapped. In the country, Mandy became energized; Allie became choked. Was it okay or even normal to not love home, to not love Oklahoma?

Mandy had parked the new van outside the old burned-down farmhouse where they had both grown up. Allie had gotten out of the van and walked toward the only remaining remnant of the burned-down farmhouse, a raised concrete foundation. Mandy had ventured behind where the house once stood to look inside an old, bleached white chicken house. After peering inside the chicken house, Mandy had run, like an un-caged colt, into the backyard towards the cellar where she, as a child, used to slide down the cellar door in her new clothes, ignoring all admonitions from an angry grandmother who issued threats and spankings to children who tore new little tomboy clothes sliding down rusty cellar doors. No number of spankings given to Mandy, however, had managed to stop her from using the cellar door as her personal slide.

Next, Mandy had pointed out a tree that lay growing on its side, "Do you remember how we hid a treasure map somewhere beneath that tree?" she had asked Allie.

Allie could not remember any of the things her sister found so endearing, and it became clear to her that her sister, though fully grown and a mother herself, hadn't moved much past being 6 years of age, at which time her grandmother had died, leaving her to explore the farm alone. Why had so many years had to pass for Allie to notice this? What had so occupied her precious time; her own private preoccupation with her wounded life and how to escape it?

Leaving Mandy by the tree, Allie had walked back to the farmhouse foundation. It looked so small that she had decided to pace it off to try and figure out how many square feet it had been. Teetering uneasily as she walked along the concrete block foundation above the old basement, now full of water and tree limbs, she walked 24 steps one way and 34 steps the other way. She called out to Mandy, "Mandy, how much is 24 times 34?"

Mandy, so bright that not only could she calculate in her head, but also she had figured out what Allie was asking and had yelled back the answer, complete with commentary: "It was 816 square feet; small wasn't it?"

Yes, it was small; it was smaller than Allie's one-bedroom condo in Atlanta. How had the three of them, Allie, Mandy, and their mother, survived in 816 square feet?

"Did you count the bathroom?" Mandy had called back.

No, she hadn't counted the bathroom; it almost didn't count; had almost never felt like a part of the house. It had been a recent addition by their mother after Grandmother had died. Specifically, it had been a closet converted into a bathroom, which Mother had given some form of style by installing pink fixtures with grey tiles, very hip colors back in the 50s.

How could the house have been so small when it had seemed so large growing up? Grandmother had always complained that the house was built wrong; that convict labor had built the house; that they couldn't read floor plans and had built the house too small. The entire back porch had been a mere half-enclosed room where Grandmother had set her rusty buckets full of turnips and squash picked fresh from the garden; the other half was destined to become the closet-turned-bathroom.

Mandy, approaching the house where Allie had stood, momentarily preparing to fire up the marijuana pipe again, had, in her confusion, misplaced the grenade lighter, so focusing her attention again on the chicken house, she motioned to Allie, "Come over here with me."

The two had approached the falling-down but locked-up old chicken house, and while looking inside the dusty windows of the chicken house, Mandy had seen something inside that made her scream with delight. "Look at those old windows," she had said. "God, Allie," she had said, "We hit the mother lode!"

Allie had peered inside, expecting to see pirate chests full of stolen gold coins, but all she had seen was an old wooden sofa frame with springs sticking up like unruly electrical currents with remnants of straw-looking horse hair still clinging to some of the coils. But, Mandy had been looking in another direction, so turning her gaze to match her sister's, Allie had seen the windows: tall, thin and covered with wasps nests.

Mandy had whipped out her phone and dialed. "Mother, Allie and I are at the old chicken house, and I found some windows I really want. Can I take them out?" After a brief time she said, "They are covered on the outside with tin, so there wouldn't be holes in the chicken house, no."

Mandy hung up the phone and with a burst of energy, exclaimed, "Let the demolition begin."

Allie had helped Mandy carry the windows to stack in back of Mandy's van; first there was a demonstration as to how the van door would automatically open from a button pressed 50 yards away. On the way home, Mandy would also demonstrate how the passenger's seat heated up on chilly autumn nights, and as they drove back home over country roads in the dark, Allie, leaning her head on the warm neck rest had watched mute trees file past them along a country road that despite sporting new, fancy, updated green street signs, had not changed one bit.

That particular trip home had left Allie within two dollars of being broke, and it was Mandy who suggested she hit up Aunt Selda, a childless widow with plenty of money, for a loan of just enough money to get her back to Atlanta. Mandy had even driven by Aunt Selda's house and, pulling all the way forward in the circular drive, left the motor running. "Scoot," she said to Allie, "Go in and ask her. What could it hurt? She's got more money than god."

Walking up the front porch steps, questioning why she hadn't visited with her aunt earlier, Allie had tried to picture Aunt Selda's face when one just shows up asking for money.

But money had always been Aunt Selda's calling card. Aside from generously shelling out money, Aunt Selda wore a harsh demeanor – puzzling to all children not privy to what the aunt must have been like as an innocent child before life intervened. Allie had only known her as someone who hid behind family money: the making of it, the hoarding of it, the doling it out in trade for perceived control and punitive disdain.

Allie had knocked on Aunt Selda's door and waited for a seemingly long time before old Andrew creaked open the door.

"Andrew!" Allie had thrown up her hands in preparation to hug Andrew's neck even as she had done as a child. He seemed much, much older than before, the lines between mouth and nose having become encrusted crevices, a depository of too much sun and chewing tobacco.

He had frowned into the night and called out as if blind, "Who is it?"

"Andrew, it's me, Allie." She could tell that his eyesight was more hindered by the random assortment of natural causes than by the time of day.

"Who? A-l-l-i-e? Miss Allie, is it? You come in here, Miss Allie. You come in here ret now." He had stretched forth his feeble arms and hugged Allie, nearly picking her up off her feet. Andrew, adopted Indian, found by the roadside back during The Great Depression, adopted by Allie's aunt, comfortable from her father's oil money, brought him home and gave him a fine life as a country- style butler, subjacent to the likes of plucking chickens, mopping floors and cooking his famous cornmeal pancakes in the old black iron skillet over the kerosene stove.

Allie had stepped into the quiet, dark foyer and heard Mandy turn off the ignition. "Andrew, it's so good to see you." Andrew had bowed his head in honor and nodded while he seemed to stand at attention. "Is Aunt Selda still up?" she had asked.

Andrew had jerked his head toward the library doors, tall wooden structures decorated with large carved Japanese Beetles, "She's in there. She's been waitin' on you," he said. "You go on in. She be happy to see you," He said, shutting the front door.

The walk toward the library, though short, had felt insurmountable – there crept in that fear of never being able to quite bridge the gap between Aunt Selda and her big desk that faced the library door. Allie had pushed open the door to the room, cold with its smells of dust resting on stockpiled money.

Aunt Selda appeared to be napping in the desk chair, checkbook sitting, ever posed, on the right side of the desk within easy reach of her veiny sleeping hand. Allie knew very well that the accompanying ink pen, when idle, always rested in the hollowed-out wooden groove built into the top center drawer of the desk, both of these things able to erase all pain except that of loneliness and lack of love.

Allie had tiptoed at first, knowing when awakened, Aunt Selda might inflict, first, vapid banter to preface each timid encounter and dreaded entry into the library. Next, before the check was written, there might fly forth a series of harsh scoldings and various penances dutifully assigned to atone for such foolish expenditures as the $40 haircut, the $100 highlight job, or the $30 lip gloss from Sephora.

Hoping this time would be different somehow, Allie had gently shaken Aunt Selda's frail hand, "Aunt Selda?" The old lady had awakened so suddenly as if to suggest she had only been posing. She had even smiled.

"Allie, your Mama told me you were here. I knew you would come to see me," she had said.

Feeling extremely guilty, Allie had known she might have skipped this visit were she not broke; she was here mainly because she needed money. Although she loved her aunt, she had never been able to find a way to express her love in a way acceptable to Aunt Selda. There would never be a way to explain to Aunt Selda that she, Allie, had ultimately failed to understand the perplexity of silent love, that there was no easy way to bridge mammoth gaps between the creatures who needed hugs and tawdry declarations of raw emotions versus the humans who could simply say, 'call me next time you are in town and I will cook dinner and give you money to get back home' and call it love.

But Allie had lied: "Aunt Selda. I couldn't come home, no matter how short a visit, and not see you."

Instinctively, Aunt Selda had reached toward her checkbook. Opening the center desk drawer and retrieving the pen, she had begun to write, speaking while she wrote, "Here's a little something for your trip home," never mentioning that there had been no request for money. The unspoken plea had hung in the air like a pronounced rain cloud.

Ripping out the check from the checkbook, she had handed it to Allie across the desk, letting her tired smile fade and her face return to stone, "I reckon I should go upstairs and go to bed," she had said.

Such huge guilt had gripped Allie that she had approached the desk as if approaching the judge's bench. She had reached out and taken the check, but not wanting to turn around until between them the air had been made clear, she had walked backwards until she had felt the doorknob poke her in the back.

All of these visits had ended the same way: nothing

meaningful being exchanged except money; each time hoping for a final absolution, but never receiving it to her satisfaction. And in what way was that? Hoping Aunt Selda would make the first move and say something sappy like, "It's okay; I can afford this; you are more to me than a liability; you are my niece whom I have loved like a daughter; you possess qualities that money cannot buy." Might she ever say, "I love you, Allie. Your mother loves you. We all love you."

Allie had turned toward the door and with her hand on the doorknob, she had wondered if she were to turn around very quickly, might there be a ray of sunshine squeezing through the heavy drapes even though the sun had set? Did reality enter into this, the squeezing of broken hearts? Might there be an aunt's confession that she was not always this way, a melting away of lines drawn when she was 8 years old and chubby and wore her cowgirl boots to school and got made fun of by classmates who taunted her and caused her heart to freeze over? Might there be one last-ditch effort at transparency that gave way to restraint? Or even, once outside the library, the heavy door securely shut, might her aunt rest her head on the desk and vow that next time, or soon, before either of them died, this gulf would be traversed once and for all?

Allie had been at the door about to walk out when she turned around abruptly to face her aunt, "Thank you, Aunt Selda."

The aunt had pursed her lips, looked down and grunted when suddenly, grabbed by a pressing urge, Allie had found long-repressed words tumbling out of her mouth, "I love you, Aunt Selda!"

Without looking back, Allie had bolted out of the library and shut the door. She had stood outside the heavy door and pressed her head against the old wooden Japanese Beetle-decorated planks while raucous tears spilled down her face, making crayon tracks in her $39.99 rosy peach blush. Allie the coward! She was the one who had failed everyone, not Aunt Selda, not Mother, not Grandmother in her too small farmhouse. Allie was the one who had left home in search of the phony ebullient parodies passing in fairytales for love. Trading diamonds for straws, Allie-the-stupid had spent half her life sifting through weeds while vacuously uprooting precious flowers all along the way.

Back in Mandy's Van, Allie had not been able to stop crying, and Mandy, well-versed in enigmatical family dynamics, had never uttered a word all during the ride back home.

CHAPTER
Seventeen

Back at the condo from the morning walk, Allie has done nothing but think about her sister and family back home. Maybe something is wrong. Maybe she needs to take a long weekend and fly home. There are plenty of sky miles to spend; probably could swing a free ticket. She will wait until 9:00 a.m. Central Standard Time, call home and discuss with her mother plans for the next trip home.

When she looks at the phone, she realizes by the blinking red light that there is a phone message and she realizes she hasn't checked messages since her concert date with Jim.

The message goes like this: "Allie, Richard here. Hope you had a good time last night. You probably did 'cause you aren't home yet, you bad girl! What'd you do? Stay out all night? Nah, nah, nah, nah, nah. Anyway, call me; I need a favor."

In most other circumstances, Allie would not call anyone on a Saturday before noon, but she knows Richard has been up since 6:00, maybe 5:30. She dials and he answers on the fourth ring.

"Richard," she says.

"My, my; took you long enough to call me back to volunteer to help me," he laughs. "Afraid of some hard work, are you? Having some fine times are we; some fast times at.."

"Richard, shut up!" says Allie, "What's going on?"

"Well, what's up," says Richard, "Is: do you remember Mark?"

"Mark in Savannah? Of course I remember him; him with the starving Koi fish and the Jackson Pollock painting?"

"Yeah, that guy," says Richard. "Seems he is liquidating his assets and moving back to New Mexico."

"Why is he doing that!" Allie is genuinely shocked, but a combination of incipient restlessness and general disquiet over the life she is about to leave behind prevents her delving deeper into the matter. "Oh, never mind," she says. "Of course I will help you out; what do you need?"

Richard continues as if he never intended to answer her question anyway, "Mark is having this gigantic estate sale."

"That's smart of him," she says, "It'll save on his moving expenses."

"Exactly," says Richard. "He is enlisting every friend he knows and every enemy who ever ticked him off, to pitch in and help."

"Sure," says Allie, "I'll help."

"This thing is going to be huge," continues Richard. "He is selling the carport, the shed, the Koi..."

"He's selling the fish?" she asks. "How do you sell fish?"

"He has already placed an advertisement in the paper," says Richard. "Trust me, this is going to be huge; it's quite the commitment."

Now, pure nosy curiosity enters the equation and she asks, "Why is he doing this? What has happened?"

Richard sighs, and sounding slightly annoyed, says, "I'm not sure I even know; I didn't ask him. I just volunteered us to help. Are you able to help; or not?"

"Of course I'll help," says Allie. "It sounds like fun, actually." She stifles her next comment, heard first in her brain and then threatening to come out verbally: I'll just let Jim know I'm going to be out of town for the weekend. "I'll just let them know at work I'll be leaving early Friday," is what she says instead.

That's good," says Richard, "I'm glad you are up for it; I'll call him. We'll leave Friday, noon."

"Can we make it about 2:00 p.m. instead?" she asks.

"Sure," says Richard, "Why not."

Hanging up the phone, Allie sits in the living room, the lamps not yet turned on for the day, yet, the sun sends a shaft of light through bamboo slats onto the whimsical painting of two colored ships Allie and Jim discussed on their first date, the painting that prompted Jim to turn around after he had seen them and say to Allie, "We have a lot in common."

Allie packs a small oversized handbag with a couple of

crushable (travel clothes they call them) things that won't wrinkle. She walks by the pictures, the curtains recycled from Aunt Selda's 1950s drapery material that hang at her bedroom windows. This was the little home she made into a haven from hurt after Bob died. The process was gradual; first came the sofa, purchased at a resale shop of overstock 'very high dollar furniture from California' had said the salesperson. Then the paintings were selected, rejected, hung and rehung until the mood of the room became consciously brighter, less brown, more alive, like a holographic rebirth in living color.

Hoping that she won't forget to call her mother and arrange a trip home soon, she dresses for the day and heads out to do errands before her next trip out of town. How is it that the productive hours fly by while the lonely ones linger on like bougainvillea vines in late Fall?

The message she will leave on Jim's phone will probably say something like: I'm helping a friend hold this huge garage sale. It will probably take a couple of days, but I hope to see you soon. I had a great time at the concert. The message she will leave on Mother's phone will probably say something like: I can't believe how much I miss all of you. Do you believe I often wake up in the night and ask myself why did I move so far away? What was I looking for? I forgot what I must have been looking for because I can tell you this: I never found it; not really. Yes, I found a new man; I like him; maybe I love him; I probably would have never met him had I stayed in Oklahoma. Maybe that is why I moved away, to meet him. Does God have anything to do with the decisions we make? Did He maybe whisk me here on a cloud, promising I would know more by and by? I hope that isn't what He intended because it is now by and by and I am no wiser.

CHAPTER
Eighteen

The weekend of the garage sale is a full moon, which is considered auspicious for 'getting rid of things.' When Richard and Allie pull up in front of Mark's house, it becomes obvious that the sale is extensive and very well organized. Garden planters, rockers, and white wicker furniture line the wide front porch. A tall palladium trellis leans against the wall and an iron firewood holder serves as a quilt rack with three or four brightly colored quilts draped over the sides. All four walls of the outdoor shed sport huge For Sale signs; and inside the shed, clothes, shoes, pillows and garden supplies line up in straight rows. Everything has a price tag on it.

After the second knock at the door, Richard and Allie are met by a smiling, thin man wearing only shorts, as if he has not had ample time to dress. When he sees Richard, his smile widens and while looking at Allie, Richard says, "Allie, this is Mark's friend, Gordy. He is also here to help out with the sale."

Crinkles around Gordy's smiling eyes give him a kind, childlike countenance. He reaches out his hand, which Allie takes; then he pulls her in for a brief hug. "Allie," he says, "very pleased to meet you."

"Nice to meet you, as well," she says.

"Thank you so much for helping," says Gordy, his voice a

deep baritone, surprising for such a compact man. Not exactly short, just thin, tall in stature, yet small in build and so nice as to seem completely non-threatening, Gordy makes it easy for Allie to like him instantly. "Thank you both," he says again, "we can certainly use your help."

"You are so welcome," she says, "Besides," she shrugs, "I owe Richard a favor or two." But then she laughs because she knows she and Richard have been inseparable since Bob died. It has nothing to do with helping and everything to do with life support.

She looks down at her blouse and sees spots that were never apparent before today. Brushing the spots, as if to brush away permanent stains – why else might the garment have been donated to Goodwill – she adds: "Who am I kidding? I'm always doing Richard favors."

"Hey, listen to you," says Richard. "It goes both ways, ya' know."

"I'm sure it does," says Gordy as he closes the door. "No one knows that more than I do."

"I must admit," says Allie, "it does."

Ahead of the two of them, Gordy sweeps his arm into the kitchen as if to take flight and fly throughout the house, tending to the details of the sale. Allie sees that the kitchen is entirely for sale. All of the cabinet doors are open and dishes are stacked up and priced. A price tag on the refrigerator, the stove, the microwave, the kitchen nook bistro table and four chairs are also priced. Napkins, tablecloths, CDs, vintage poodle and deer planters, small lampshades, books and a few VHS tapes all sit atop the bistro table.

"Wow!" says Richard, "You guys are ready!"

"That we are," says Gordy, calmly.

Richard gestures toward the VHS tapes, "Really? Do you think someone is seriously going to buy the tapes?"

"One never knows," says Gordy, "One never knows."

Mark comes into the kitchen; he hugs Richard, then Allie. "Thank you both," he says. "I think we are going to be extremely busy this weekend and I truly appreciate your help."

Mark turns around and begins walking toward the large living room and as he does, he motions his arm forward, indicating that Richard, Allie and Gordy should follow. "Let me show you sleeping arrangements," he says.

As they walk through the living room Allie sees the Jackson Pollock painting leaning against the sectional. In fact, the entire leading wall has been hung, floor to ceiling, with artwork, a price on each piece. Tall bookshelves are virtually crammed with books, knick-knacks, candle holders, small picture frames, stationery, envelopes, ballpoint pens, staplers and paperclips.

The sight prompts Richard to comment, "Man, Mark, where had you been keeping all this stuff? Your house seemed so sparse before."

Mark shrugs his shoulders, laughs a little and says the old proverbial, "You never looked in my closets" line.

"Also, the shed," says Gordy, "He had a lot of stuff in the shed, too."

"Yes," says Richard, "But, the shed is full as well. At least, I thought it was full. Shows you how much I know."

"Now you know!" says Mark, "This is precisely why I needed your help; and I appreciate it very much."

When they reach the back bedroom at the far end of the house, Mark says, "This is my bedroom; but, you're welcome to shower in the bathroom there. We'll just have to take turns, that's all."

Allie doesn't like showers: the water beating down on her head. Admitting this would be as passé as an admission that you still have dial-up so she says, "That is no problem for me. I'll take the bathroom with the tub. That will be one less person jockeying for the shower."

"No, you don't have to do that," says Mark.

"No, but I will," says Allie, "I insist; end of subject." She laughs, the subterfuge cleverly skirted.

The next room, a middle bedroom, is completely empty except for brand new Berber carpet on the floor, "Gordy has agreed to sleep in here on the floor," says Mark.

Richard looks at Gordy, "Sure you want to sleep on the floor?"

Gordy nods, "I prefer sleeping on a hard surface. Anyone who knows me knows I am a complete minimalist."

"If you are a true minimalist, all that stuff in the living room must be driving you crazy!" says Allie.

"On the contrary," says Gordy. "It will please me to see it go bye-bye, one picture frame at a time."

They reach the front bedroom, windows open, breezes blowing white sheer curtains straight into the room. "This," says Mark, "will be Richard's room." A blown-up air mattress sits center of the room directly in line with the breeze. Light and airy, the room resembles a hotel room where Allie once stayed while vacationing in Monte Carlo on the French Riviera, back, way back, when she dated an older man. Odd, how time and the tricks time plays has the devilish ability to transport that same 23-year old girl waking up in a French hotel room overlooking the Mediterranean Sea drinking champagne in the morning listening to a working French carpenter with a beautiful tenor voice sing "O sole mio" while he clanged pipes, into the present time (some 22 years later) to a large beautiful house in Savannah, Georgia, which is up for sale along with everything in it. Same girl, different age, same tom-foolery, different house, different country.

"And Allie," says Mark, "you get the sectional and I hope that is okay."

Not once during this tour has she thought about where she will sleep; the sectional will be fine. It is positioned directly beneath the ceiling fan, which will be a cool and comfortable snooze; she can sprawl out and still have the rest of the sectional to drape across it the few pieces of clothing she has brought in hopes of selling in the sale.

Through the open window she sees a couple of people walking a dog. An elderly woman works in the yard down the street, her lawns sprinklers going full blast, and, it is with a bit of regret that Allie believes she sees migratory birds flying south.

CHAPTER
Nineteen

The first morning of the sale Allie positions herself at the edge of the garage on a folding lawn chair with a big cardboard box in front of her to use as a desk. She has brought a calculator, a pen and a clipboard filled with blank paper. Such organizational preparation proves to be a good thing, as people start coming early in the morning. All four of them, Mark, Richard, Allie and Gordy have items for sale, so drawing four columns down the paper, she labels consecutive columns in alphabetical order: A, G, M, and R. During the flurry of sale activity, this will be an easy way to keep the money separate, since she is also keeper of the bank that Mark has prepared with several ones, fives, tens and one twenty dollar bill.

The first customers of the day, a family consisting of two grown teenagers, both of them girls, an elderly man, and a hugely obese older woman, pull into the yard and get out of the truck. They walk into the garage where Allie sits behind the box and Gordy sits on one of the white wicker rockers that he has stolen from the front porch.

"Good morning," says Gordy.

"Mornin'," says the obese woman, "Hot 'nuff for ya?"

"Yeah-ha-ha," says Gordy. He rocks back and holds the rocker still with his feet.

Allie gestures behind her, "There's more stuff in the house."

"They is?" the woman looks toward the house.

"Yes, LOTS more stuff," says Gordy.

There are more things for sale in the shed, also" says Allie. She beckons toward the yard, away from the carport, and the woman looks behind her.

"I'm lookin' for cherubs," says the woman. "Got any cherubs?"

"Probably," says Gordy, "Just go on inside and look around. I think you will find this is not your average garage sale. It's more like an estate sale."

"Someone die?" asks the woman,

"Not really," says Gordy, cryptically.

As the woman goes into the house to join the man and the two teenagers who have preceded her, Allie hears Mark greet them.

Another couple of cars have pulled in and both cars appear to have three or four people per car. Soon, the garage is full, the front porch is full, and the house is full of people. They start bringing things out into the garage to pay while Allie instructs them to stack them aside and she will 'wrap and sack.' Making up little sales tickets for each sack, she keeps their purchases straight, systematically separated.

People start bringing in tools from the shed, and, one

woman asks Allie, "What size are the clothes out there?"

"The clothes are size 6," she says, "And the shoes are size 8."

A couple of more cars pull in and one of the customers says, "I came to see the Koi that was advertised in the paper."

"Oh, the Koi," says Allie. Encouraged, she looks to Gordy to help answer the question.

"Here," says Gordy, and, he stands, "Come with me. I'll show you the man you need to talk to about the Koi." Gordy starts into the house, with the woman trailing behind him.

While Gordy is inside the house, a man walks over to Allie, points to large rocks surrounding a tree in the front yard, "Are them rocks for sale?" he asks.

"Ah," says Allie, "I'm not sure. Tell you who to ask; go inside the house and ask for Mark; he can tell you."

"Okay, thanks," says the man; he walks past her and into the house.

Soon Gordy comes out and sits back down in the wicker rocker. It seems evident to Allie that this tiny bit of human interaction begins to wear on him. He winks, his eyes a slit, "I have a little smoke for later if you're so inclined." Allie smiles back but says nothing.

"I'm going to need it, I can tell you that," he rocks back and lays his head on the back of the rocker.

"This is actually kind of fun for me," says Allie. "It's good to get away from Atlanta once in a while." In the saying of that she realizes the hypocrisy of the statement. In actuality, she is ALWAYS getting away from Atlanta. And now there is Jim, whom Allie wants to know better, faster; wants to become comfortable being around him; be ever excited to see him; excited when their hands touch, when they hold hands: all the stuff of fairytales.

"Well, more to the point," she says, "not get away from Atlanta so much as just to get away from much of the humdrum that makes up so much of life," she clarifies.

"Where do you go to get away from that? Please tell me because I want to go there too! No, I hear you," says Gordy, "I think it might be good to get away from Atlanta a lot of the time."

"Yeah, but," says Allie, "I like Atlanta; I really do. It has everything: theatre, ballet, good restaurants. It's difficult to navigate sometimes, though."

"Yeah, traffic!" says Gordy. "I moved away from Atlanta; moved out to 40 acres."

"Where do you live?" she asks. "I live on 40 acres outside of Macon," he says.

"Sounds nice." Allie watches him stare down a darkening sky.

"Yep, after I had cancer twice, I moved on to a simpler life and I haven't looked back; haven't regretted it a bit," he says.

Startled by the cavalier manner used to introduce such a

serious subject as cancer, Allie struggles to remain shock-proof. "I should think not," she says.

"Cancer was my wakeup call," he says. "I was forced to look at my thoughts, and I realized I was angry about a lot of things."

"Angry at things? Like what things?" Allie wonders if this is rude behavior to quiz him, so she adds: "Not that it is any of my business."

"No," says Gordy, "It's okay. I've thought about this a lot. One of the things I was angry about was plants, of all things."

Allie squelches the impulse to laugh, "Plants?" she asks, "As in house plants? Mad at plants?"

"Well, not all plants, just intrusive plants," says Gordy, "Plants like Kudzu and Wisteria, plants that take over landscapes, all intrusive plants, I was ticked at them; really ticked."

As mesmerizing as it is how a low-profile, seemingly kind individual like Gordy could on the one hand be so amiable, but on the other hand be so hostile at something so innocuous as a plant strikes Allie so funny that she loses the battle with the suppressed giggle and breaks into a loud and embarrassing round of inappropriate laughter.

Gordy stares straight ahead while he continues, "My graveyard headstone should probably read: ANGRY."

Allie senses he is angry even now. "Oh, I am sorry," she says.

Still rocking steadily in the chair, he smiles at the sky, "Don't be," he says. "I understand; it's ridiculous. But, that's just the thing about feelings, especially illogical ones: who knows where they come from? And, they don't have to make sense, do they; they just are."

"Yeah, well my graveyard headstone should probably read: BORED," she says. She glances over to see if he is smiling, but, he is still stone-faced looking out past mountains and trees.

Practicing a bit of back porch psychology, Allie asks, "Did you ever make the connection that maybe intrusive plants represent a larger intrusive something-or-other that makes you angry?"

"Oh, no doubt," he says. "Believe me, I did all kinds of soul-searching, and the fact remains, of all the things to be mad at in this world, intrusive plants really piss me off; still do. But, I try to let it go; it isn't worth it. I've made progress. These days I'm fairly laid back." His expression remains inscrutable.

"I can sort of tell," says Allie, "in fact that is one of the things I instantly liked about you: your easy going nature."

Gordy blows wind through his lips, which give way to a sort of laugh when he says, "easy-going nature; I like that. I must remember that."

Allie doesn't know if he is being sarcastic or humble. She clears her throat as if to utterly change the subject just before a woman approaches the make-shift cardboard desk holding a few of Allie's own clothes in one hand and a pair of her shoes in the other.

"Will you take $3 for these shoes?" the woman asks.

What do I have on them?" asks Allie, momentarily annoyed at the garage sale for taking priority over meaningful conversation.

"You have $5," says the woman, "I also want this blouse and this pants suit."

"Okay," says Allie, "Three dollars on the shoes; everything else is as-marked."

The woman pays and walks away while at the same time the obese woman and her family come out into the garage with armfuls of little stuff. They set them down beside Allie where she tallies the total, and Gordy jumps up to wrap them and sack them. They pay and leave.

Walking ahead of the woman who came for the fish, Mark walks from the house, through the garage, and they continue on toward the privacy fence, which leads to the back yard. Allie flashes a wide grin at Gordy, "Oh, I hope they sell the Koi! Find them a good home; I worry about them!"

"Why?" he seems puzzled.

"Because that time Richard and I went to visit Mark, the fish seemed hungry to me; starving, in fact," she says.

"No, they feed off of algae," says Gordy.

"But, you should have seen them," she persists, "they would actually jump out of the water when I walked out onto the deck!"

"Koi are very friendly," says Gordy, and again, Allie fights to stifle the urge to laugh. Why is Gordy so funny?

He continues, "They are social fish; they are very much like dogs in that respect. They were probably just coming to greet you."

That does it, Allie throws back her head and laughs the way she laughs at Cow and Chicken cartoon, which displays the cow's udder as typical breast implants: with all four teats sticking straight out. "Are you saying the fish are jumping out of the water, endangering their survival to come and say hi to me?"

"No kidding," says Gordy. Allie suspects for a moment that he is just placating her; trying to make her feel better so she won't worry about the fish much as he shouldn't trouble himself over intrusive plants. He continues, "Koi is just a kind of an overgrown Goldfish. They are very much house pets."

In awe of these minute morsels of knowledge a country girl should know but doesn't, she marvels at having grown up on a farm ever ignorant of the intricate details of intrusive plants and Koi fish.

People proceed forward with loads of items in their hands: the spoils of the house. They don't barter; they just pay. Obviously, Mark has marked stuff cheap enough that they are willing to buy. More cars pull in and go inside the house.

The dogs in the backyard are barking at the strange woman who is invading their domain and threatening to take away their Koi companions.

With time nearing 4:00 p.m., the sale obviously waning, the garage, now steaming hot from the heat of the day, which heat has become unbearable to Gordy, he moves, rocker and all, onto the front porch, positioning the chair to sit in the shade of the overgrown Camellia bush. He pulls out his marijuana pipe and begins to smoke, blowing smoke toward the east, daring and be- damning the neighbors and the garage-sale customers to say a damn thing about it.

Separating their money four ways, Allie, parched and hot, plans a nice bath where she will sprinkle in some lilac bath crystals, salvaged from the sale, just as Richard steps down into the garage.

"I'm getting hungry," she says to him.

"We all are," he says. "In fact, Mark says to close up the sale. We're going to the neighbor's for a drink."

"Did the lady buy the fish?" she asks.

"Only a few," he says.

This is her worst fear: lonely fish, forgotten fish, unloved fish, fish left to starve, rejected fish. What will happen to them when Mark moves away?

"Only a few," she sounds alarmed, "What will happen to the rest?"

But Richard's priorities are not Allie's priorities, and he continues, his mind more focused on the evening ahead than on the plight of the fish, "Don't forget," he says, "Mark is asking $25.00 a fish."

"But!" Allie persists, "he has hundreds of fish! Where will the rest of them go if they don't sell?"

"Calm down, oh ye of little faith! Maybe he'll sell them all. Also, this is just the first day of the sale; we're hoping someone will come along, buy the rest, and while they are at it, buy the pond, the equipment – the whole nine yards." Richard steps back up onto the step that leads into the kitchen and yells, "Anyway, shut it down; close the door. Let's get dressed for cocktails."

Feeling particularly unsociable, Allie would rather go off alone like a dying lobo wolf and have dinner at McDonald's or Olive Garden, someplace safe and cheap and homey. "I'm so tired; but mostly I'm hungry and thirsty! Gosh, I'm so thirsty!" she says.

"That's what I'm saying!" Richard sounds almost impatient, "We are going to Mark's friends' house at Tybee. Go! Take a bath. Go out in the shed, grab one of the outfits you brought for the sale, get dressed. Let's go!"

The futility of becoming suddenly anti-social at this multi-family garage sale event announces she'll have to go, like it or not, over to Mark's neighbor's house and act like she is having fun when she really only wants to go eat, crash on the sectional and call Jim. It is clear, however, that tensions seem high and she is going to have to placate everyone, a quality she has mastered with expert agility.

"All right," she stands and begins to gather together the change dish, the calculator, the tablet drawn with vertical lines.

Richard steps back into the house, and she walks toward the shed that houses the clothes she has brought to the sale. One of the dresses, a little black cocktail dress with a pearl-studded neckline and cutout sides that lay bare the shoulders, a dress she bought once to use as a Halloween costume, will do. Show them and their: have to go to the neighbor's and have a drink attitude! She'll go, in costume, as Audrey Hepburn, short of donning black gloves and carrying a long cigarette holder. She will wear her hair up, she'll wear the tight black sheath with pearl neckline and sleeveless bodice. She doesn't know these people after all; will probably never see them ever again, so why not dress for the occasion.

Water filling the bathtub, she calls Jim and while it rings, steps, phone and all, into the water. Reclining in the tub, water up to her breasts in hot, lilac-scented water, she carefully holds the phone with one dry hand, and they talk. Jim misses her, he says; he is making very special plans for their next date; it is to be a surprise so he won't tell her a thing; she'll have to guess; and also he adores her.

CHAPTER Twenty

Mark's neighbors live in a house on Tybee Island, which is an attached villa with a good vista. It faces the Atlantic Ocean and the top level of the house sits high up so as to afford an unobstructed view of shrimp boats and jumping dolphins. Downstairs, people sing big band songs which have within them hopeful lilts common to days acquainted with more simple times: days before the Twin Towers were ravaged and before the financials were raided – times that now seem almost innocent.

Mark handles the introductions of his neighbors, Rickie and Glen, a middle-aged couple, who Mark said had once worked for the FBI. Rickie had been a secretary when she met Glen; however, Glen's line of work was largely 'skirted.'

As Mark begins the introductions to Richard and Allie, it becomes clear these neighbors already know Gordy because while Mark is introducing Glen, Rickie immediately begins to speak with Gordy about oyster season and how it is right around the corner.

"Allie and Richard," says Mark, "please meet Rickie and Glen."

The couple looks alike, as couples often do who have been together for a while: Rickie sports a very short haircut, although she is not a small woman. Rather large, she wears big round owl-like glasses the color of gold Bakelite. Behind the glasses, her eyes appear sharp and knowing. She stares at Allie and says, "Pleased to meet you," but it is obvious that Rickie only has eyes for Mark, and is delighted to see him because her eyes follow his every word and they gleam and sparkle, as eyes do when they behold their beloved.

After the introduction, Rickie sips from a frosty glass, then gestures the glass toward Allie as she speaks. "Let me make you a drink. What would you like?"

Before Allie can answer, Glen steps forward and stands squarely in front of Allie. "Wait a minute," he says to her.

He offers his hand to Allie, and looking at her while he addresses Mark, he says: "Mark have you been keeping pretty little secrets from me?" Then he lowers his head and looks directly, almost uncomfortably dead on, into Allie's eyes, "I bet I can make you a drink you will like."

"Oh, Glen," Rickie swats him on the shoulder, "Knock it off."

So here they are, Mark's neighbors: a couple, obviously bored with one another, the wife with eyes for her gay neighbor, the husband with eyes for anything wearing a skirt, pride themselves in making good drinks.

"Pleased to meet you," says Allie. Glen continues to look at her and continues to hold her hand.

"Who is singing downstairs?" she asks.

It sounds as if there is a live band in the house, or it could be just unusually loud canned music. Slow and steady now, the downstairs music, having abandoned big band songs, now features music that progresses nowhere, like jazz, consisting of the same few notes which ramble on with no destination in particular. Right now, she could be anywhere: Atlanta, the French Riviera, California; the music matching precisely the predicament: anything goes anywhere.

"Is that a local group who is playing?" Glen looks at Rickie and asks, "Who are they, again?"

"The Lobos," Rickie says, "The Low Country Lobos. You like them?" Raising her eyebrows, she smiles at Allie.

Allie pulls her hand from Glen's grasp, "Yes, I do. I love music."

Rickie steps forward now and positions herself between Allie and Glen. "Glen, let me make her a drink. I have a good one in mind."

It is obvious Rickie harbors no hard feelings, nor does she feel threatened by Glen's forward behavior. She turns to Allie, "What do you like to drink?"

"Actually, just some cold water; it has been an awfully hot day for a garage sale," says Allie.

"Oh, yes, the sale," says Glen, "We heard about the sale." He steps back into the circle and begins to check out the short hem of Allie's dress. "I like the dress," he says.

"Thank you," says Allie, feeling her face beginning to redden. Why had she even agreed to come to the neighbors' house? But, specifically, why had she insisted on wearing a dress that was once destined to be a Halloween costume.

"Your dress reminds me of a dress Audrey Hepburn wore in Breakfast at Tiffany's," says Glen.

Bingo. On the nose he recognizes it; he is correct. "Yep, the sale!" Allie diverts the conversation away from attire and back to libation. "It was hot and I am parched, but I don't really drink the hard stuff," she looks at Rickie, who seems shocked.

"What do you mean? You don't imbibe?" Rickie turns around, mid-drink, Vodka in one hand, a whole lime in the other. "Seriously?"

"Well, not the hard stuff, anyway," Allie says.

"Oh, no," Rickie is determined, "I have the perfect drink. It is very mild. You will love it; I am making you one!"

"What is it?" asks Allie. Outdone by thirst, music and by newly found friends, she wills her resolve to crumble. Hypnotized by the sea, by the music, she looks at the wall of windows, misty now with evening and ocean spray. Soon it will be September: early nights, cool mornings, drabness relieved by leaves turned red and gold; birds will desert the landscape; later, cold will leave fountains to freeze over and icicles to form on house eaves. She misses her family back in Oklahoma; misses them almost more than she misses Jim, the latecomer to the fairytale. There were loves before him and he is the newest. That is his role in all this: Jim, the newest love.

"I call it my lime freeze," says Rickie.

Glen has not moved from the circle. He stands and listens as Rickie petitions Allie.

Mark, Richard, and Gordy are now no longer in the room. Maybe they are in the bathroom; maybe downstairs. Maybe they are in the kitchen munching on hors d'oeuvres.

"It's light, I promise," Rickie continues, "You will love it; it is made with lime-flavored vodka and lime juice."

"It sounds delightful," says Allie, "It honestly does. Okay." With that, she will sip the drink; she will find the boys; will find something to eat; will explore the house. She might slip away and call Jim before it gets too late. Maybe she won't.

Drink in hand, Allie and Glen walk downstairs to join the party in obvious full swing. Dishes of nuts and candies sit on tables and a large pool table has been set with finger food: sandwiches, vegetables and dip, toothpicks of fruit and cheese, chips and dips, chicken wings, hummus and pita, cupcakes, sliced gyros.

Homogeneous and friendly, this crowd differs from the South Carolina beach crowd as far as can be geographically contained on such a small map. If South Carolina was the "old money" and this is the "new money," this party presents a dance-til-the-plague-takes-over frenzy. Cigarette smoke fills the room and the atmosphere is loud and happy like it is in certain restaurants at Phipps Plaza.

"You allow people to smoke in your house?" Allie asks Glen.

"Obviously," he sets his drink down on a china saucer sitting on a table beside a large teal leather ottoman.

Allie looks down at her dress. The black hem stopping just above the knee, a wide white pearl trim sewn around the neck of the black sleeveless sheath. She feels ridiculous, as she is much more overdressed than these rowdy people who wear jeans and flip-flops. They, who know full well that leverages have leveraged-out, that million-dollar ocean front mansions are worth half that now, that property sits preened for, at best, repossession, and at worst, auction, obviously care nothing any more for leverages; they merely breathe air that is heavy with surreal resolve. The music, still jazzy, progresses, like the crowd: nowhere. Progression being no longer the point, there comes a time in every tragedy when hope deferred becomes out and out comedic chaos, and this party beautifully attests to that.

Relaxing among the noise, Allie sips on the lime freeze. Delicious and soothing, it goes down easy, satisfying not only parched thirst but the taciturn heart as well. A few people are actually playing pin-the-tail-on-the-donkey, their eyes blindfolded while they run towards the wall with a big pin with a donkey tail attached to it. Laughter follows when the attempt ends in one person falling over a large overstuffed chair.

"So, how do you know Mark?" asks Glen

"He is a friend of a friend; he is Richard's friend," she says, "And I know Richard. I know Mark only through Richard."

"Oh, yes, Richard the decorator," says Glen.

"Is that what you call him?" Amused, she thinks of Richard as her best friend, partner in crime, confidant, adopted brother, fallback pal, the last resort, but not as decorator.

Glen raises his glass, "Let's drink to decorators and beautiful women."

Allie looks down, then around, then over her shoulder, in search of beautiful women.

"Don't be so coy," says Glen, "You must know you are beautiful. In fact, you look like –"

"I know," she says, "You've already told me: Audrey Hepburn!"

"You get told that a lot, don't you?" says Glen.

"Sometimes," she says. "Not a lot. I think it's just because I'm skinny with no boobs, to speak of."

Well, these days," says Glen, "that can be solved."

"Oh, I really don't want big boobs," says Allie, shocked that she is opening up to Glen this way. "Besides, don't big boobs cause back problems?"

"Oh, you've got a lot of years left before back problems are gonna set in." Glen suddenly surprises Allie by jumping up on the ottoman and waving his drink into the thick air, "Look everybody. Look who joins us tonight: Audrey Hepburn."

The music continues, crowd noises rise, a few people stop what they are doing and look, but mostly they go on about their very important business of enjoying the evening.

Allie sips the drink. True to her word, Rickie has made a

delicious drink: light, the teeniest bit addictive; she raises the glass toward Glen, "I would like to propose a toast to fun parties and happy people."

Glen steps down from the ottoman and clinks her glass with his. "I would like to add to that a toast: to beautiful days and good food, two of the pleasures left in old age, with beautiful days continually abundant but good food receiving a moratorium once the Primary Care Doc gets involved."

"Whatever." Allie clinks their glasses together, and they both take another swig.

"Here," says Glen, "Let's sit." He leads the way past the pool table, picking up a cheese-laden toothpick as he passes and pops the cheese into his mouth; then, he flips the toothpick back onto the felt-lined pool table.

They settle by the window and Allie can feel cool air creeping in near the glass. The drink makes her feel tipsy. "Glen," she says, "What do you think your graveyard headstone will say?"

He frowns and holds his drink in midair, "I'll have to think about that a bit." He takes a sip. "Probably something like: Here rests Glen, willing annual judge of the Naughty School Girl Contest."

Allie spews lime-flavored vodka on herself and laughs at the visual. Wiping liquid from her mouth, she brushes droplets from her dress. "Enough said," she raises the cool drink to her lips again and drinks.

CHAPTER Twenty-One

It is going on three weeks past the infamous garage sale, and on a clear cloudless morning, cool for early September, perfect for jogging, Allie runs out of the house, garbage in hand, which she will deposit in the bin, then continue her run past the elementary school, and then past the house on the corner, newly up for sale, its sunflower garden bending over and turning brown beneath autumn's scrutiny. Then, she will finish her run past silent Confederate soldier graveyards.

The countryside is fast becoming colored with gold, red and green leaves a full week later than that of the North Georgia Mountains. That had been the surprise date Jim had planned: a trip to the North Georgia Mountains.

How beautiful are the mountains in the fall season: haunting, misty, mysterious. The mountain people are pure, simple, hollowed out and uncomplicated, compared to city people. They reflect their scenery: honest, sparse, yet lush in their own simple way.

Jim had rented for the weekend a room at a quaint bed and breakfast, owned by a married same sex couple who allowed two dogs to frolic freely in the front yard without restraint of leash. Not once did they see any other guests, and, for that matter, they didn't see much of the owners either, because Jim and Allie had slept late and lingered in the bed making love and missing breakfast.

During the day they had indulged in their favorite pastime: junking, and at night, they sought out different downtown restaurants in nearby Chattanooga.

One day while driving up Lookout Mountain, Jim had pointed off, right of the road. "What is that?"

Allie had looked out the passenger window to see a huge opening in the side of the mountain. Taking advantage of the wide roadside shoulder, Jim had pulled over and parked, and the two of them had sat gazing at the opening for a long moment before Jim had decided to check it out. "Let's get out and see what that is, exactly."

They had gotten out of the van, cars wheeling past on their crane up the mountain, leaving mountain dust which had risen from road concrete in a slow-motion haze. The two had walked to the opening on the side of the mountain and gone inside.

Essentially a cave inside a mountain, the place had been as quiet as a tomb except for the faint sound of dripping water. Once inside the mountain, the air had instantly become 10 to 15 degrees cooler, and Jim had put out his arm and pulled Allie closer, where, huddling together, the temperature inside the cave soon became more comfortable.

"I have to get a picture of this," Jim had said. "Let's go back outside.

Taking Allie's hand, he had led her back outside of the mountain into the warm autumn sun. "Back up and let me focus you in the camera," he had said.

He had held the camera up, peered through the lens and said, "Wow! Your hair looks like a halo."

I like the way your sparkling earrings lay…

"Next to your pale skin; it is such a lovely contrast! You should see it!"

…against your skin so brown…

"This would be a romantic place to make love," he had said.

…and I want to sleep with you in the desert tonight…

"You, me, the golden leaves, the dripping stream."

…with a million stars all around…

He had lowered the camera for a moment and had said, "Allie, this feels so right, being with you."

…cause I get a peaceful, easy feeling…

"I feel like I have known you forever," he had continued.

…I know you won't let me down…

"Somehow, I know we're in this for the long haul." He had let the camera flop against his chest, all intentions of picture-taking temporarily on hold.

…'cause I'm already standing on the ground…

He had walked toward her as she stood by the cave entrance

and with strong arms and big workman's hands had encircled her body, holding her like a fragile figurine, and when he bent down to kiss her, she tiptoed up to meet him halfway.

Allie runs past the second leg of the condos where she lives, which, one by one, are being sold short, foreclosed, or auctioned off for pennies on the dollar.

Her own condo is paid for, courtesy of Aunt Selda, yet most of the young couples who bought condos at the height of the real estate frenzy are now gone, despite the new school, the easy access to public transportation, the safety of the neighborhood: none of it matters anymore. The rules have changed and no one knows exactly how the new rules should read.

The morning air bodes eerie, given this new absence of joy. Window blinds are closed in house after house. If life is being lived behind darkened windows, isn't that the same as life being lived underground in a bomb shelter? No one seems to move behind shuttered openings, where lights have gone dark, where ancients sleep, where phones have been superseded by e-mail. Even the Confederate soldier graveyard seems more of a refugee camp with this new pall hanging about the atmosphere; it is as if the very earth holds its breath.

In comparison to the majesty of the mountains, such nonsense now seems utterly trivial, so much so as to not merit an ounce of deliberation.

She turns the corner at Goldie Drive and runs up the hill away from the Confederate soldier graveyard. The rest of the run will be used to offer a prayer into the midmorning for all people, meaningful or trite, for all soldiers, living or dead, for all lovers, glossy in their need to find peace for themselves during the expanse of their lives upon the earth.

Once inside the condo, Allie decides to clarify her thoughts about Jim by writing them down. Sitting at the computer, she creates a document, entitling it: DEAR THIRD HUSBAND.

She will merely stream of consciousness at first, just to get the thoughts on paper; then she will edit them.

She begins: Dear Third Husband:

I'm sorry I failed you by wasting all that time not speaking to you. I was afraid of being hurt, I guess. Maybe I was afraid our love might have blossomed, bloomed, and then died, as so many loves do. And, it might, still. We would have had magical days to remember along with dusty days, as lovers do. In time, the magical days might have shone more brightly while the dusty days might have crumbled, eroding more each day until only dust would remain and then be blown away by winds with the power to scatter dust.

I'm sorry I held your hand and endured your first kiss on my cheek with hesitation and doubt. Such scrutiny lives side-by-side along with all lovers who would reduce their spark to a litany of wrongs: too many eggs in the meatloaf, too few flowers in the vase, too many football games on television, too many breakfasts at Waffle House.

I'm sorry if I bypassed your offer to open car doors for me. I should have stepped into your coach, lifting my petticoats;

revealed a glimpse of my glass slipper as I stepped into your pumpkin. You would have gently eased the petticoat, tucked it inside the door frame, and would have stolen a kiss before you shut the pumpkin door. On the ride to the ball, you would have reached across the coach, smoothed my hair as you often do in bed after holding me close. You would have said in small gestures how, across time, you found me; that despite my initial resistance, you embraced me.

I'm sorry we met late in life before children. Beautiful children they would be: you with your navy blue eyes and beauty mark on your check which you say is a scar but I say is a dimple, me with my Audrey Hepburn jaw and resolve, you with fair Irish full head of curly silver hair, me my gamine reluctance and brown eyes the color of dark garnets, you your strong hands and arms. Their beauty would have sunk ships and leveled mountains, our children: virtual cause of chaos in a sleeping world. Their sun would have eclipsed this tarnished world of rain. I'm sorry for beauty lost and glory squandered. And, I wonder if I will ever send this letter to you.

Allie puts down her pen and begins to make plans to return to Oklahoma, a visit far overdue.

CHAPTER
Twenty-Two

"Work is largely unnecessary, you know," Wendy says to Allie while they sit outside on the patio of Café Intermezzo and sip tea.

Wendy is Allie's friend from the neighborhood, one of the remaining few who still has a job and owns a condo. She is also famous for being able to escape life's new atrocities by attending chick flicks.

"Work is," Allie struggles to formulate clear sentences that effectively define work, "work is inconvenient, I know that for sure."

"Work is play if you love it," says Wendy, "but then, my dear, it no longer becomes work; it becomes play."

"Well spoken," says Allie, "well-spoken and adequately thought out."

"So when are you leaving for Oklahoma?" asks Wendy.

Allie had begun to dread trips back home once they broadcasted a perpetual loom of defunct life plans and dreams positively shimmering in their mockery. Home begged the unanswered question of why did you leave? Home had become the holographic shadow that refused to abate, the Greek Chorus that continually chanted: when are you coming back, when are you coming back? You've accomplished nothing but flight; when are you moving back? Allie decides with not a moment's hesitation to tell Wendy about her new love.

"Wendy," says Allie. "Can I tell you something? I think now that I can never move back; can never move back home."

Wendy looks over her raised cup of tea, which framing gives her eyes new focus so as to register more clearly her surprise at hearing this, the final admission she has suspected for all the years she has known Allie. She speaks, "You realize don't you, that you have not made a mistake by leaving home."

"No," says Allie, "Not exactly. You see, I still feel and will probably always feel, will go to my grave feeling, that I deserted everything and everyone who really mattered in order to chase a dream which I have never managed to give a name."

Wendy leans back in the wrought iron chair. Setting the cup down on the umbrella-covered table, she looks at the tree across the parking lot. Cars whizz past them on the way to various places, and although it is September, the sun shines and bounces off the pavement, warming the morning to near-perfect room temperature. "Allie," she says, "you are too hard on yourself."

"I know." Allie has heard this phrase all her life. She takes a deep breath and continues, "Wendy, the reason I cannot go back home is that I think I have met my third husband."

Wendy, who believes in happy endings and who refuses to see practically any movie other than those rated PG, doesn't bat an eyelash, but leans forward, both arms on the table, and says, "Tell me everything."

"Well," begins Allie, "I haven't told anyone but you. I've hinted around, but no one really knows the scoop. It's so simple. Basically, we have known each other for 10 years."

For the first time Wendy seems startled. She straightens in her chair a little, taking her arms off the table and sits at rapt attention, "Who is it? It's someone I know, isn't it!"

"Not really," says Allie, "He doesn't travel in our circles. You wouldn't know him, I don't think. You see, considering me and my flea-marketing addiction, seems he and I both have the same affection for junk. Besides that, we seem to end up shopping at the same stores on the same days!"

"You mean you met him shopping flea markets around town?" Wendy seems shocked.

"No, I actually met him officially at the pet store," says Allie.

"Now, I'm confused," Wendy picks up her cup and takes a sip.

"Simple," says Allie, "I kept bumping into him over the years when I was in all my various second-hand haunts, and then one day we just happened to be in the same pet store where he finally introduced himself."

"Oh, Allie," says Wendy, "This is just so meant to be! I'm getting goose bumps."

"I figured you would," says Allie. "Richard thought he was a stalker and Elyquia hasn't even heard about him yet, but I knew you would understand."

"Understand? I do indeed!" says Wendy. She raises her cup in the air, "Let's drink to love."

The girls clink cups, take sips and set the cups back down on the table. Wendy continues, "No, you definitely cannot move back home; not now, anyway."

"I think you understand my conundrum," says Allie.

"Don't tell me you are even entertaining the thought!" Wendy scolds.

"Not really," says Allie, "I think I'm just using the dilemma to beat myself up."

Wendy throws up her hands, "Of course. Would I suspect otherwise?" She looks firmly across the table, "Allie, you could use a good brain transplant. Maybe that would help."

"Maybe," says Allie.

The Café Intermezzo is next to a newly opened, high-end men's shoe store that used to be a hair salon before it went belly up from lack of customers after the big fall. Slowly, the façade of the little town square is changing. More families are walking; there seems to have been an explosion of young moms jogging while pushing baby buggies. Families who once bought huge SUVs now find themselves stuck with the expense of those gas-guzzling vehicles. Mercedes and BMWs have virtually disappeared. The intrusion of lean economics upon the heretofore megalopolis feels like a brewing storm whose timing feels pitifully incompatible with blossoming love. A girl should hold onto her lucky fortune with everything she's got!

When the women drain the last of the tea from their cups, they stand, hug goodbye, and after they walk to their separate vehicles, Wendy turns and waves, the sun upon her face giving her angelic translucence. "Drive carefully, sweet friend," she says.

"You too," says Allie.

CHAPTER
Twenty-Three

Practically family tradition, the first chore to be accomplished once Allie reaches Oklahoma is to visit Walmart with her mother, who, ever unable to hide her joy at seeing her oldest daughter, pushes the grocery cart past mountains of tempting baked goods, asking Allie, "Would you like some of these muffins?"

Her mother holds a package of large blueberry muffins with both hands and delicately displays them as if presenting a valuable proffer beneath the Walmart canned music canopy of Jim Reeves, who sings "Welcome To My World."

"No, Mother," says Allie, "I have almost completely quit eating wheat."

Her mother sets them back on the stack. Instinctively, Allie knows she should have said yes, because her mother wants them; she likes to treat herself when Allie comes home.

"But, please," Allie attempts to soften the blow of her self-absorbed intent, "Mother, go ahead and get them; they'll be eaten. It's just: don't buy anything special for me. I can always find something to eat." Her guilt feels leaden now because she clearly sees how two people try to communicate while saying nothing they really mean. "I..I really might eat one; go ahead and get them."

But her mother, moving slowly forward, advances the

grocery cart toward the produce aisle, "Maybe some fruit. What kind of fruit do you like?"

Basically kind and strong, her mother is gracious and she struggles with how to act; struggles with how to soothe the prodigal daughter so she won't run away from home again. Allie wonders if, after years of being gone from home, she has encouraged her mother's renewed resolve to reconnect, to answer questions, as old as the decades, which questions may, by some miracle, bridge the gap.

Suddenly, she yearns to cry and to bring out into the open the "it" that hangs in the air like a mist that will not materialize.

"Mother, truly, get what you like; or, Dad, what does he like?" Allie feels more guilt every second, with her tendency to, while trying to save the fuss, ends up denying her mother's pleasure.

"He doesn't eat much of anything these days," her mother shrugs, "mostly soup and toast."

Allie knows that, in her mother's mind, food equals love. If only she had a healthy appetite. The family story goes that when she was born, Allie tried to starve herself; wouldn't eat. It was the grandmother who had saved her; forced raw eggs down her throat day after day until she finally began to eat something: mostly sweet things. The spiritual explanation of this family tale might be: Allie, born into her own self-imposed dismal existence, wants to die. Thereafter, food became the catch-all default folder.

It is late, time is ticking, yet she has never found a way to close the gap once and for all. But, she wants to. She wants to say the truth: Mother, I don't know what is this mist. Why your guilt? Why mine? All I know is that we do love one another. We've just never been able to say it.

Allie wants to break the silence and say it out loud; wants to shout it above the Walmart music: "let's go back in time, you and me; let's change our life's events and let's rewrite this unfortunate outcome; let's un-decide the decisions that set me on this lonely journey and left you with your pensive questions. Both of us have sacrificed: you have the hillside country you love, but a link is missing from your peace of mind. I have the city I always thought I craved, yet I ever sport this huge, unplugged hole in my heart."

Allie's guilt at leaving her family behind to the quiet of the country hangs on her year after year like a shackled garment, threadbare and soiled. Its persistence colors every event, spoils every occasion, torments every silent conversation; the albatross never goes away. Ever present, this redundant, growing, flaring, infected piece of flesh has won the prize. It has prevailed as the winner, beating out ambitious plans, mighty dreams, and all intentions, both good and bad.

"I know what let's do," says Allie. "Let's get something different; let's get a pie. Have you ever eaten Key Lime Pie?"

"I don't reckon I have," says her mother, her face brightening.

"Do you like lemon pie?" asks Allie.

"Oh, it's one of my favorites," says her mother. Her smile is sweet and oh, so innocent.

"Then, you'll like Key Lime Pie. It's a southern thing; it's made with lime instead of lemons. Also, there isn't as much wheat in the pie crust as in the muffins," says Allie. "It will be healthier for us."

"Ok." Her mother eagerly lays the pie carefully into the shopping cart.

"Sure you are okay with that?" asks Allie.

"Sure," says her mother, " Dad might even eat some too."

They walk back towards the dairy case, which holds also Cheesecake, Boston Cream Pie, Custard Pie and other refrigerated baked goods. Allie, who walks faster toward the case than her mother, looks over her shoulder and sees her pushing the cart, holding the handle for support, bending over the cart, surveying its contents as if counting.

An American Flag hangs vertically over the Walmart Vision Center Section in celebration, no doubt, of the upcoming Columbus Day holiday. Only two or three people sit inside the Vision Center waiting for their glasses to be made.

She swallows tears, as an old James Cagney movie flashes in her mind. In the movie, Cagney's character had tried to be a good son; had tried to be a success, but by the end of the movie, everyone, including him, knows he had failed. He continues the ruse, however, as he climbs to the top of the highest building in New York City, where everyone, including Cagney's character, knows he is going to die. They know he has been putting on an act all these years; has been putting a fake smile on his face.

Climbing to the top of the building and just before firing into the tank, yells… "Made it, Ma! Top o' the world!"

"Oh, you like this cheese, don't you?" Mother holds up a large, round Brie. "I remember when you went to France. You came back and you loved this cheese." Tentatively, she sets it into the grocery basket, watching Allie the whole time.

"You're right; I do love Brie. Let's get it." her mother really has been listening all these years; has been searching for a way to connect, whether with the right foods, whether with living vicariously through the ridiculous trips to Europe, the gambling junkets with careless boyfriends. In her way, Allie's mother has been there for her daughter, holding onto the frayed connection with everything she had.

Allie reaches out and stops the shopping cart with her hand. "Mother, I am so sorry that I have never been there for you."

"What do you mean?" her mother grins when she asks the question. "Of course you have been there." She will never admit her pain. Maybe she has never recognized her pain.

Surprised, she continues, "What do you think you are doing right now? You're home, aren't you? You've come home to see me, haven't you?"

Allie looks down.

"You're visiting me now. I know you're busy in Atlanta," says her mother.

"Not that busy, Mother, not really." Allie struggles to dredge up one noteworthy accomplishment she has realized with her life, other than that of trailing through art museums in Italy, drinking champagne in Monte Carlo hotel rooms, shopping at leather outdoor vendor carts in Florence, Italy. Who do I think I am? Is anyone really home in his dense head? Anyone home? Heartache is my handle. Sheer heartache.

"Well, I guess I've just never had the luxury of thinking about what you are saying," says her mother, "I've always had to work like a dog."

There it is: the anger, the righteous anger. It's about time! Allie breathes silent relief. She removes her hand from the cart so her mother may push it forward, rendering the vehicle half cart, half walker. She knows how easily misunderstandings can evolve into arguments; the knowledge relieves her guilt.

Her mother points down the aisle, "I don't want to walk all that way; would you walk down and get me two jugs of Arm and Hammer laundry detergent?"

"Sure," says Allie.

"Get the liquid," says her mother, "and get the one that says Fresh Burst."

"Okay." Walking down the laundry detergent aisle, Allie passes women pushing over-loaded shopping carts. There are families with children, there are husbands wearing cowboy hats, there are people with too much belly fat, unaware of the health dangers that lie ahead, carting around all that belly fat. Obviously, food promises to make the world a better place. What soon shall become of this ravenous society, braced to go from zero to eleven in five seconds? There was the Oklahoma City Bombing; there was Nine Eleven; there were beheadings: trauma all over the world. Maybe Allie's mother had earned the right to be afraid that her daughter might have suffered one of those awful atrocities that happen in the big city; while, all the while, Allie might have earned the right to be afraid that she would be 1,000 miles away when her mother drew her last breath.

Allie brings back two large containers of laundry detergent, too heavy for her mother to lift. Like it or not, it is on the horizon: soon her mother will need perpetual help during these shopping outings, while Allie will be traipsing around Atlanta going to parties, holding garage sales, visiting holes in mountains, going to rooftop concerts in ballgown dresses, finding enough love and peace to finally lay this body by.

Gently, she places the laundry detergent down into the center of the shopping cart. Maybe this trip home isn't going to serve as the resolution of past aches; maybe it can only serve as a dutiful trip. Surely duty counts for something on the daughter scale.

Making their way slowly toward the checkout counter, she and her mother line up behind six or seven people who appear to be buying out the store. Within the vast expanse of Walmart, half of the town is shopping here because since Walmart took over, all the Mom-and-Pop stores have been run out of town: plumb out of town. Allie boycotted Walmart for years because of that.

CHAPTER
Twenty-Four

Back at the house, Allie unloads the van while her mother carries two sacks, her back bent beneath their weight. They walk past her father and two of his friends, who sit out under the tree, smoking and talking. The men discuss the tractor that was stolen from the hayfield; how it was probably driven all the way to Mexico, where it would likely be broken down, part by part, and sold. Odd, though, "wouldn't you think someone would notice a big green John Deere tractor driving down the highway?" they laughed.

"But the tractor had sat out in the pasture with the keys still in it and all," said one of the men.

"I reckon some migrant worker probably be plowin' the corn fields somewhere in central Mexico about rat' now," said another.

The men marvel at the ease of pig farming: how pigs will eat anything, so you could just stack pigs on top of one another and only bother to feed the top pigs because they would poop and the pigs beneath them would just eat the poop: create a trickle-down effect, like Reaganomics.

The three men laugh, one of them flips his cigarette out into the field, unafraid of wildfires because the ground is saturated from all the rain they have had lately. In fact, a thunderstorm appears to be gathering on the horizon. Lightning might strike and they might lose power, but farmers are always prepared to lose power.

Aunt Selda's husband, although he would have never considered himself a farmer, would certainly have been prepared to lose power. Uncle Raymond, good Lieutenant Major that he was, well-trained by the Army, steward of useful things like battery-operated lamps for times such as when the electricity went out. He would be prepared for the storm ahead.

Allie has Uncle Raymond's lamp back in her condo in Atlanta. So many times she had tried to sell the lamp in various garage sales and consignment shops, yet the lamp would never sell. Any money the sale of the lamp would have generated toward her constant search for money remains a moot point now, seeing as how it sits, non-vendible, available on stand-by, ready to light the condo in case of powerful storms.

Allie and her mother begin to put the food away into the three refrigerators in and around the house: one in the kitchen, one on a patio outside, and another in a barn-type shed outside, alongside a freezer that stands in front of long rows of canned food, some of it jelly that was canned in 1979, likely to be needed some day if the Great Depression ever came again.

Looking out the kitchen window, Allie sees that the yard is littered with rusting tools, with falling-apart coolers, with broken concrete planters. An old refrigerator sits in the carport, its door hanging off, and with dirty contents hanging out the front of it. There are cats in the yard: so many because they have been left to breed to such abundance that very often one of the dogs will eat a litter of kittens. Two of the cats are blind, their eyes having been scratched out in fights.

Allie opens the kitchen door and calls, "Here, kitty, kitty."

An old cat, upon hearing her voice, crawls out from under one of the sheds, using his front paws only, as his hind legs appear to be paralyzed. He lies on the grass in full sun and with what sounds like last breaths, he meows very weakly to Allie. She opens the kitchen door, walks over to the cat until she can see that he is skin and bones; sees that he has an oozing sore on one side. Both of his eyes are clouded over, like a blind eye would cloud over, and there is pus in both eyes.

Allie runs back into the house, and while her mother is busy putting away the bread in the bread box and the laundry detergent on top of the washing machine, she pulls from the refrigerator some of the food that will often sit in the back of the refrigerator until it spoils so much that even an animal won't eat it. She retrieves a fat chicken breast and also pours a large bowl full of milk. She goes back outside and hand-feeds the lame cat, one bite at a time, until he has finished the chicken. Then she holds the bowl of milk to his lips until he drinks it all. Allie is surprised at his appetite. He may die on her watch, but at least he will die with a full stomach.

The clouds overhead threaten more rain, which will feel like God's tears on her face. Allie had planned to tell her mother about Jim, but now that revelation has slipped to the back of the line because, suddenly, it seems not only distractingly unimportant, but insignificant in these barren, basic survival prairie fields. She feels as if she is walking on land mines, with the object of the walk being to get through life with as little trauma as possible. Her most pressing assignment is to get back to Atlanta as soon as possible, to call Jim and tell him how much he was missed, and then to let her own fat black cat go outside where he will, no doubt, sit looking at the grass as if to survey his options: do I bask in the sun? Do I chase a squirrel? Or, do I just roll around in the dirt?

The farmhouse screen door slams and in walks her sister, Mandy, squinting through a stream of cigarette smoke that trails up into her eyes, since she holds the cigarette firmly in her lips while she struggles with a small dog wiggling in her arms.

"Mandy!" Allie runs toward her sister with outstretched arms.

Mandy releases the small dog, and it immediately runs into the front room where it begins to sniff the throw rug in front of the couch.

"Lucy! No!" Mandy yells. "I have to watch her; she loves to pee in the house." Mandy walks into the living room and talks very sweetly to the dog, "Do you need to go outside?" She turns to Allie, "Excuse us." Placing the cigarette back between her lips, she stoops down, picks up the dog and heads back toward the screen door.

"I'll come with you," Allie follows Mandy and Lucy, going back outside. Once her feet hit the ground, the dog breaks free and runs toward the chicken house. Mandy waves the air, "It's okay. She loves to chase the chickens, and they are still cooped up so let her go."

"Let's go around front and sit on the front porch swing," says Allie.

They walk around to the front of the house, climb the steps and sit on the swing. It sways a couple of times as they sit, but soon it settles.

"Mandy, why don't you gather up a bunch of these poor cats and take them into town to get neutered?" Allie asks.

Mandy blows forth a stream of cigarette smoke as straight as a jet stream cloud, "I just can't deal with that kind of pain anymore," she says.

"What pain?" asks Allie.

"The pain of worrying about all of these neglected animals. That's part of farm life, Allie." She looks at her sister.

"But, what about the poor cats' lives?" asks Allie,

"That is Mom and Dad's problem," says Mandy.

"I can't stand to even think about them," says Allie.

"You don't have to," says Mandy, "You aren't here! You're in Atlanta!"

"Oh, I still think about it though," says Allie. "I feel horrible guilt. More than you can imagine. What do you think I have in Atlanta? This great big glamorous life?"

"I never think about it," says Mandy, she, the softie in the family, who has managed to build an impermeable wall around the core of her heart where no teardrop shall see the light of day.

"Well, I don't, except that," Allie hesitates while her dad and his two buddies slowly make their way to the house. Dad, stooped more than Allie remembers, adjusts his hat, holding it by the bill, twisting it left and right until it perches on his head just the way he wants. He waves at the girls then tucks his thumbs inside the loops on his overalls; he talks in muffled tones to his two friends, their voices fading more and more, as the three of them approach the back of the house.

Allie continues. "I have met this guy in Atlanta."

"Have you?" Mandy flips her cigarette onto the concrete porch floor and stomps on it, swaying the swing as she rotates her foot.

"Yes, I really like him; he is husband material; might be my third husband," Allie says.

"Good grief," says Mandy. "Have you told Mom?"

"No, and I may not," says Allie.

"That's probably just as well," says Mandy.

Lucy, back from peeing in the yard and chasing chickens, jumps up on the porch and whines. Mandy reaches down and lifts her onto her lap. The dog circles a couple of times, then finds a comfortable lap position and lies down. The girls swing in silence and look at small hills on the horizon. Some people say those hills were old Indian burial mounds, though no one ever officially confirmed that, however. Folklore and old family stories mull and mix themselves together, swirling around like tornadoes.

"So, how are you doing?" Allie asks her sister.

"I'm fine these days," says Mandy. "Basically, I just sort of want people to leave me alone."

"But won't you be lonely?" Allie asks.

"Yeah, probably." Mandy looks across the dirt road at an old house built of planked wood that is falling down, collapsing under years of rain and prairie wind. It is sitting on some farmer's land: a patch of land safe from strict city zoning regulations. If the house wants to fall down, it can do so without any governmental scrutiny whatsoever.

Allie looks at her sister and remembers a happy, freckle-faced sibling who once chased her through the house completely covered in mud. Mandy was the tomboy; Allie was the prissy one, screaming because she was about to be attacked by a mischievous little sister holding handfuls of freshly brewed mud.

"Do you prefer being lonely?" Allie persists.

"I don't know; maybe, for a start." Mandy looks back from across the road, "And what is this? The Spanish Inquisition?"

"No," says Allie, "It is the Sister Inquisition."

"Yeah, well," says Mandy, "there is no such inquisition."

"Maybe I'm starting one," says Allie.

"Maybe I'm shutting it down," says Mandy.

They rock on the swing in silence. Four o'clock and the shadows it brings begin to make their evening sweep, a dreaded time of day for Allie. Four o'clock signals the end of something, which mornings usually redeem.

"How is Aunt Selda?" Allie asks.

"Same," says Mandy, "You should really go see her."

"I should," says Allie. "I really should. I just feel like she always thinks I want money when I go see her because she always writes me out a check."

"Well," says Mandy, "she thinks of us as her girls. You know, she never had any children. We were her kids. She misses you a lot; you should really go see her."

"I will," says Allie.

Their mother calls from the back of the house, but they continue to swing in silence, both of them aware of not only the dangers of time and distance, but also that of the ticking clock. How long ago was it: that Christmas when they cut their own trees from their own pasture? Another year, their Christmas tree nearly touched the ceiling. Their trees were decorated every year with lights that looked like bubbling tubes of liquid.

Christmas celebrations aside, there was another fond celebration memory, and it was of Mandy's 12th birthday party, which was an overnight pajama party in the loft of the hay barn. The menu was deviled eggs, Pecan Sandies, pimento cheese sandwiches, and celery with peanut butter.

Next came the birth of their children: one son to Mandy and one son to Allie, both boys who, being raised in the midst of women, grew up to be well-honed on how to exhibit compassion toward women, children and small animals.

Mother calls again, her voice sounding closer now. "Where are you girls?"

"We're coming, Mother," says Mandy. They stand and she motions toward Allie, "Go see Aunt Selda before you leave."

"Promise," says Allie.

CHAPTER
Twenty-Five

The flight arrives late at Hartsfield-Jackson International Airport in Atlanta. Although she could take Marta, Allie opts for a cab. She is tired, almost depressed, and wants no drama. She leans her head on the seat and watches street scenes as the taxi makes its way onto the expressway, where a young man stands beside the exit dressed in a red, white and blue striped jumpsuit, holding a large sign that reads: JESUS LOVES YOU.

Okay, Allie, you can relax now. You only seemed to have lost your way because it has been difficult to be you: so impressionistic, so easily imposed upon. You know very well your inner secrets of confidence and faith? Isn't it a fact that each man knows his own true way? You simply never believed in yourself; you must begin to do so. Going window shopping in the stores of life is most distracting; sooner or later, one must settle for something. To your son's little friends, you were the woman with the mean face, who answered the door in a nightgown, standing in a darkened foyer. To the naive men in the world, you were sweet, mean, beautiful, ugly, available, elusive…who cared? To Mother you were a sickly, pitiful child. To Aunt Selda you were a vivacious, social butterfly. To casual onlookers you might be smiling, frowning, radiant, dark, confident, insecure. But, to yourself, you are an incorrigible recluse, as ineffectual and grounded as a one-winged butterfly, who can spend an entire week pretending your life is a movie. And should you write your own obituary, it might read like this:

"A Star was found frozen in the snow on the streets of Atlanta in an obscure subdivision of million-dollar homes built on top of Confederate soldier battlegrounds. Police are asking how she died. Did she die of a broken heart? But, more importantly, the people of Atlanta are asking why was this Star found overlooked and free-floating on the streets of Atlanta? Was it because she never made it to Hollywood where she could have died with the proper pomp and ceremony worthy of celebrity status, to be played out on television screens all across America? Perhaps the answer lies with the falling leaves, the snowflakes, the GA 400 roaring traffic. They know the answer to the riddle and it is this: some Stars are hand-picked to huddle in canals and cradle the lone. Some Stars are reserved to merely serve, and their number is mighty few indeed. Take care whom you entertain, it could be a Star unaware."

People don't have to do much to make a difference. Consider the teacher in Oklahoma, who, after the tornado, kept her kids distracted from the oncoming danger of the tornado by having them sing the Battle Hymn of the Republic, regardless of the fact that our very Republic seems to be crumbling beneath our feet. We are all over the place; our only uniformity is fighting. One would think we were two foreign countries living under one disgruntled umbrella.

Memories of home remain the same, yet the glaring truth of the aging memories is this: what had once been considered fineries are merely broken-down remnants, moldy cotton quilts, and sagging antiques. Those items, once revered by the family as valuable and protected by the family as such, are mere relics no longer sought after in auction houses across the country. When you moved to the city, you created a life for yourself (such as it was). To have stayed on the farm would have been to accept the life that was created; whether that life might have become suffocating doesn't figure in here. No, you fixed all that with your dreams and your busy, busy, busyness. What better way than chaos to distract from loneliness? You distracted yourself with motion, which often passes for progress. Activity quiets the unloved soul, even though the quality of activity is entirely inconsequential, because all loneliness gets buried beneath the fiery flames of turmoil. Our family's love has merely flown; risen like the coal mine canary higher each time through trauma upon trauma. We have run like the gazelle through tall grasses, over the cliff into doom valley, day after day, time upon time. Too much love lives in our being. One understands such love that has nowhere to go, so we dance. We kill, then we die from anguish over the loss of the very thing we chase: double homicide, double suicide. No one lives; no one dies; no one resurrects. Putting on more and more makeup, we only make Dorian Grey look more and more garish. THIS HAS GOT TO STOP!

Allie straightens up in the back seat and rummages in her purse for a paper and pen. She will spend the remainder of the cab ride home adding on to the letter to Jim that she will probably never allow him to read. She sees it clearly now; Jim really is her new direction. He is the future. She must find a way between now and the next time she sees him to become healthy, worthy of a successful third marriage. She writes:

You never want hate in your heart. You've said it and I've seen it. I have seen you turn your head to differences of any kind; have seen you give ear to plebeian ramblings, those times, smoke rising, eyes planning, you seldom spoke until the flower was formed; then out of your silence would appear the bouquet. That rock of sobriety, I esteem most. Staunch and steadfast, your very name means "rock." You are a humble man, with wisdom, and the one that I love.

Allie knows the truth even though she has made a life pretending otherwise. She once had a gun held to her forehead. She once narrowly escaped being abducted, only by way of having a thin dime to drop into a laundromat payphone to call home for help. She ran away from home at seventeen. She charged her way halfway across the country from Oklahoma to Atlanta using an American Express card with a $300 limit. Yet, she had never been as scared as now. Standing without representation, amidst the furniture and the sky, in an attempt to carve out a rightful place in which to belong, having the audacity to believe in personal rights never formally granted or bequeathed from an established hierarchy, she had, up to now, the courage to exist through sheer belief in her dreams, in her made-up stories!

Only now, she sees the truth: she is exactly like Lula Mae in Breakfast at Tiffany's: a fraud who merely changed her name. What was she trying to do by leaving Oklahoma? Run away to New York? Be Holly Golightly? Did she think the country girl wouldn't find her? If she were writing her own version of the movie it would go like this:

HE: Will you marry me?

SHE: It's difficult because I love Atlanta.

HE: Then, why are you leaving?

SHE: Did you find the plane ticket?

HE: You can't leave. You're not cut out for Oklahoma.

SHE: Plane leaves at 12:00, and I'll be on it.

HE: Allie, I am not going to let you. I am in love with you.

SHE: So what?

HE: I love you; you belong to me.

SHE: Driver, pull over.

HE: You know what's wrong with you? You're chicken!

SHE: I can't do this, Jim.

HE: You call yourself a free spirit. You're not a free spirit; you're in a cage!

SHE: (She gives back the ring.)

HE: No matter where you run, you will only run into yourself!

SHE: (gets out of the cab in the pouring rain.)

HE: (he gets out of the cab in the pouring rain and embraces her.)

Cue: Moon River

SHE: I don't know, Jim. I just don't know.

HE: I do, though. Please, trust me because I know. I do know.

"Ma'am," the cab driver calls to her, "what is the exact address we are going to? I want to be sure I entered it correctly in my machine."

Allie rips up the screenplay she has just written, writes her address on the back of half of one of the sheets and gives it to him.

"Thanks," he says.

She leans back in the cab seat, feeling safe, as they crawl through the inky Atlanta evening. That dusk-colored skyline coming into view is Atlanta, not New York City. And, it isn't raining, and she is not holding a cat between them while he pulls her close and kisses her in the rain. But it is going to end the same.

In her mind, she does return his kiss because this story will have a happy ending. All fairytales have happy endings.